SALVAGED VOWS

THE BILLIONAIRES OF CREST STRATEGIES
BOOK 3

ELORA RAE

First published in the United States of America in September 2025.

Cover Design by Elora Rae

978-1-953139-22-1 (Ebook)

978-1-953139-33-7 (Paperback)

First Edition

10 9 8 7 6 5 4 3 2 1

ALSO BY ELORA RAE

To everyone who has survived abuse and wants to see a man lose his dick privileges.

TRIGGER/CONTENT WARNING

Hey gorgeous (likely unhinged) readers!

This novella is a dark billionaire romance.

Before you dive into Tanner and Blair's wonderfully tense love story, let's chat about what you're getting into because we all know that in this genre, content warnings are how we choose books...

Inside this book, you'll find:
- **Domestic violence and abuse**: Including detailed depictions of past (and present) physical and emotional abuse, as well as threats and intimidation
- **Sexual assault**: On-page non-consensual sexual violence that is graphically described. PLEASE be discerning when reading chapters 13 and 14
- **Violence and blood**: Including kidnapping, shootings, torture, dismemberment/mutilation, significant gore, and murder
- **Excessive swearing and profanity**: These characters have filthy mouths in more ways than one

• **Spicy, high-heat sex scenes**: Including oral sex, rough consensual sex, and size-related content

Other content warnings: Government conspiracy and black ops activities, human experimentation, drug-induced compliance/mind control, temporary loss of agency, severe injury and medical trauma, murder and revenge killing, past trauma responses including PTSD and panic attacks, discussion of suicide, and characters in life-threatening situations.

I did say it was dark...

The good news? The relationship between Tanner and Blair is healing for both characters. The darkness comes from external threats, past trauma, and morally gray choices made to protect each other, not from toxic dynamics between Tanner and Blair. Also, the character who does the sexual abuse gets his "toys" taken away in the most satisfying scene ever.

If any of these themes are upsetting or not your thing, please take care while reading, or maybe skip this one. There are lots of amazing books out there, so find the ones that bring you joy, not stress.

But if you're here for a tense, sexy, high-stakes story where a deadly security specialist will burn the world down to protect the brilliant scientist he married out of convenience and is now falling for...

Welcome to the *Billionaires of Crest Strategies*.

You've been warned.

Happy reading!

-Elora

P.S. If you or someone you know is experiencing domestic violence or sexual assault, help is available. The National Domestic Violence Hotline (1-800-799-7233) and RAINN's National Sexual Assault Hotline (1-800-656-4673) provide 24/7 confidential support. You can also visit thehotline.org or rainn.org for resources and live chat options.

CHAPTER ONE

BLAIR

BLAIR WINTERS WAS SO SICK OF MEN IN SUITS TELLING HER she was wrong.

"Ms. Winters, we—"

"It's Doctor. Dr. Winters," she corrected, seething inside.

"Dr. Winters, we simply cannot allow testing to continue after these allegations." The FDA representative's voice droned like a lazy insect.

Blair bit her tongue until she tasted copper. Three doctorates, seventeen patents, and a breakthrough that could help thousands of paralyzed patients, yet these bureaucrats looked at her like she was a hysterical girl playing with dangerous toys. She'd spent her entire career proving herself in labs dominated by men who assumed her success was luck or affirmative action or sleeping with the right professor. Never again.

"The whistleblower report raises serious concerns about potential weapons applications."

Blair squared her shoulders, staring down the panel of five men and one woman who held her life's work in their bureaucratic hands. The conference room felt too small, too warm, with walls that seemed to inch closer with each passing minute.

"The allegations are completely false," she said, fighting to keep her voice steady. "My research has never, not once, been directed toward offensive applications. The neural regeneration properties of VX-7 have documented therapeutic potential for spinal injuries."

The woman, Dr. Clyborne from the NIH, glanced down at the report in front of her. "The molecular structure bears striking similarities to VX nerve agents. You understand our concern."

"Similar is not the same. Water bears a striking similarity to hydrogen peroxide, but one hydrates you and the other kills you." Blair took a breath, reining herself in. "The whistleblower deliberately misconstrued early test results."

"Nevertheless," said the man at the center, a representative for the Department of Defense. "All testing must cease pending investigation. Your lab will be sealed effective immediately."

Five years of research. Millions in funding. All her test subjects who were finally showing promising nerve regeneration. Gone because someone had lied.

"You can't—" Blair started.

"We can, and we have." Andrews shuffled his papers. "This meeting is adjourned."

Blair remained seated as they filed out, her mind racing through options that dwindled with each passing second. By tomorrow, this would hit the news. Brilliant Scientist Develops Illegal Bioweapon. Her reputation would be shredded before she could defend herself.

Her phone vibrated. A news alert: *Breaking: Winters Biomedical Under Investigation for Illegal Weapons Development.*

Shit. It had already begun.

———

THREE HOURS LATER, BLAIR STOOD IN HER EMPTIED LAB, security tape crossing the entrance like yellow crime scene markers. Two uniformed guards watched as she collected personal items from her desk. She'd been given fifteen minutes. Fifteen minutes to salvage something from half a decade of work.

"Dr. Winters?" Her research assistant, Constantine, hovered in the doorway. "I'm so sorry about this."

Blair tried to smile but couldn't quite manage it. "Not your fault."

"I know you weren't developing weapons," he said, voice low. "We all know."

She nodded, throat tight. "Tell the others... tell them I'll fix this."

As she left the building, carrying a pathetic box of framed degrees and family photos, Blair's phone rang. Unknown number.

"Hello?"

"Dr. Winters." A crisp male voice. "My name is Carson Crest, CEO of Crest Strategies. I believe we can help with your situation."

Blair nearly laughed. "Unless you can convince the Department of Defense I'm not developing bioweapons, I seriously doubt it."

"Actually, that's exactly what we do."

"You're a PR firm?" Blair walked faster toward her car, scanning the growing crowd of reporters near the parking garage.

"We're a reputation management company with specialized experience in crisis situations like yours."

Blair reached her car and dumped her box in the passenger seat before sliding behind the wheel. "My crisis isn't a sex scandal or some celebrity drama where someone said something stupid. My entire life's work has been misrepresented as biological terrorism. I think there's a bit of a difference there."

"Which is why I would like to meet you personally."

Resting her head against the wheel, Blair sighed.

"I don't see the point. The investigation on my life's work has already begun and just like with placebo experiments, they're going to see what they want to see and ruin me further." She snorted, sitting up and slumping with her head against the headrest. "Besides, with my work frozen, I won't be able to pay for your help."

"I'm sure we can work something out, Ms. Winters. That is," he paused, "if you actually want to fix this."

"Of course I want to fix this!" Blair snapped, slamming her palm against the steering wheel. "What they are doing is shitty and based on a lie. Do you know how many people with paralysis I could help if these idiots would just let me work?"

The billionaire, whose company had saved celebrities, politicians, and corporations from complete destruction, remained silent.

Taking a deep breath to calm herself again, Blair shifted her grip on her phone. "When can we meet?" she asked.

"How quickly can you get to Manhattan?"

Blair glanced at the reporters now recording her sitting in her car. Her phone was already flooded with notifications: colleagues distancing themselves, conference invitations rescinded, and most alarmingly, a message from her primary funding source starting termination procedures.

"I can be there in two hours."

Blair immediately began talking to herself as soon as the call ended. It had driven her ex-husband crazy when she did that, but at least it kept her sane.

"Complete idiots. Molecular similarity? By that logic, we should ban table salt because chlorine is toxic. Should I have simplified it more? Used smaller words? Drawn them a picture? God, I need to call Dr. Kustka at Cornell. He'll vouch for the therapeutic applications. And the trial patients. What happens to them now? Did the panel care about how many fucking lives this is helping? No. God, funding will freeze by morning. Five years of work. My entire reputation. Think, Blair, think..."

She realized she'd been talking out loud for several minutes, her words tumbling faster as her mind raced through collapsing possibilities. With a deep breath, she started the car and pulled out of the parking lot, ignoring the reporters tapping on her windows.

———

THE CREST STRATEGIES BUILDING TOWERED OVER THE street below, gleaming with all of its glass and steel edges. Blair stepped from her car feeling decidedly underdressed in the black pants and emerald blouse she'd hastily changed into at a rest stop bathroom.

At the reception desk, a sleek blonde woman smiled. "Dr. Winters. Welcome to Crest Strategies. Mr. Crest is expecting you."

The elevator ride to the top floor gave Blair just enough time to doubt every decision that had led her here. She'd driven straight from her lab in Connecticut without a plan beyond this meeting. If Crest Strategies couldn't help her, what then?

The doors opened to reveal a minimalist reception area where a striking woman with auburn hair pulled into a severe braid waited.

"Dr. Winters. Jenna Briggs, head of security." She extended her hand. "Thank you for coming."

Blair shook her hand, noting the woman's firm grip and the subtle bulge of a concealed weapon beneath her tailored jacket. The woman was terrifying.

"The team is assembled in the conference room," Jenna said, leading the way down a corridor.

"Team?"

"Mr. Crest has called the other head members of Crest Strategies in response to your case. Time is critical in situations like yours."

Before Blair could ask more questions, Jenna opened a door to a large conference room where four men sat around a polished table.

"Dr. Winters," said the man at the head of the table, rising. "Carson Crest. Thank you for coming. My team: Benedict Astor, operations and surveillance director," he indicated a slender man with ice-blue eyes, "and Penn Lavigne, our digital specialist." The younger man with disheveled light brown hair barely looked up from multiple screens, one of which seemed to be running facial recognition software on what looked like social media photos.

"And Tanner Whitney," Carson finished, nodding toward the fourth man.

Blair's attention shifted to the large man who was already watching her. Unlike the others in their perfect suits, Tanner Whitney simply wore a dress shirt and a tie, the sleeves rolled up to reveal full-sleeve tattoos on both forearms. Broader shoulders stretched his shirt, and for a moment, Blair wondered how much of the rest of him was tattooed. His military-short hair and the scar that bisected his left eyebrow made him look far meaner than the rest of the men present. The rotten scowl on his face didn't help either.

"Mr. Whitney handles our more... specialized security concerns," Carson explained.

Tanner's gaze swept over Blair, as though cataloging threats rather than meeting a potential client. His silence felt deliberate rather than awkward.

"We're usually a team of five, but our fifth is currently representing us in a court case. James Rothschild is our law specialist and a particularly cunning lawyer. Please, sit," Carson gestured to a chair. "We've reviewed the initial reports about your situation. Quite the mess."

Blair sank into the offered chair. "That's one word for it."

"Would you mind filling us in on what it is you've been working on?" The man Carson had referred to as Benedict asked with a reassuring nod. "It will help us determine the best way to help you."

"Right, yes. Of course," Blair tore her focus from Tanner, who was still staring at her like she'd run over his dog with her car. It was far more pleasant to look at the other three men, which was what she did. "My VX-7 compound targets damaged myelin sheaths in the central nervous system," Blair explained, unable to keep the passion from her voice. "Initial trials showed 78% neural regeneration in subjects with complete C4 spinal severance. Yes, the molecular backbone shares structural elements with organophosphates, but we've modified the binding sites to target only damaged nerve tissue. Whoever this fucking whistleblower is, they deliberately omitted the protein markers that prevent systemic toxicity."

Across the table, Tanner raised an eyebrow. However, he remained silent.

The obvious tech genius, Penn, nodded before his fingers flew across his keyboard. "The whistleblower report hit six news outlets simultaneously at 9:47 this morning. It was a coordinated attack."

"Which suggests this wasn't a concerned employee," Benedict added. "Likely a planned takedown."

Blair's stomach turned. She bit her lip. "You think someone

targeted me specifically? That's a large assumption to make without more data to support it."

"Your research has significant potential market value," Carson explained. "We've seen this sort of thing before. When someone develops something monumental, other people want credit and fame for it. Your pharmaceutical applications are likely worth billions, and defense applications worth more. Someone likely wants to control it."

"But why not just offer to buy me out? Why destroy me?"

"It's cheaper," Tanner finally spoke.

"Exactly. It would be cheaper to acquire distressed assets. Discredit you, devalue your company, and then gain the research for pennies," Carson said, nodding.

Blair dropped her attention to the table, frowning as she considered their words. It made sense. In fact, it was quite smart, even if it was ruining her life.

"Mr. Whitney has experience with similar tactics in military operations," Carson explained. "His assessment is typically accurate."

Penn swiveled his chair. "I've been analyzing chatter around your company. Three venture capital firms have shown a sudden interest in your patents since the allegations broke." His gaze flicked briefly to a secondary screen showing what appeared to be surveillance footage before returning to his work.

"So what do I do?" Blair asked, unable to hide the desperation edging her voice as she rubbed the hem of her sleeve between two fingers. "I deal with chemistry and pharmaceuticals. Biology, not... this." She gestured towards Penn's laptops.

"That's why I reached out to you." Carson leaned forward. "We can mount a comprehensive defense. Media strategy, legal counter-offensive, and most importantly, security protocols to protect you and your research."

"I can't afford—"

"We can discuss payment options later," Carson waved away her concern. "First, we need to understand exactly what we're dealing with. I need complete transparency from you."

Blair hesitated. Her research was her life. Sharing it meant vulnerability she wasn't comfortable with.

"We can't help if you hold back," Carson added.

"It's not that simple. My work contains proprietary elements that—"

"Are potentially being stolen as we speak," Tanner interrupted, his gaze locked on hers. "Every minute you waste increases the risk."

"But it's my life's work. I can't just—"

"It won't be yours for much longer." Tanner scoffed, lifting an eyebrow.

"Are you threatening me?"

"Of course not. Mr. Whitney has a direct approach," Benedict said, his voice diplomatic, "but unfortunately he's right. Full disclosure is your best protection."

Blair glanced from Benedict, whose reassuring smile was the absolute antithesis of the glare on Tanner's face. Who'd pissed in his coffee? Still though, he was probably right, not that she'd ever admit it. She couldn't deal with the whistleblower's fallout alone.

"Fine. Full disclosure." She pulled a small drive out of her bag. "This contains everything. My research, test results, molecular structures, everything. I want an NDA contract signed by anyone who has access to this."

"Done," Carson said with a nod. "I'll put James on it when he gets back to the office later today."

"I want a temporary one now, though, before I give it over."

Benedict was already writing something on a tablet, and he passed it to Carson first. "It's rudimentary, but it would hold up in court. Gentlemen, Ms. Winters, please sign."

They passed the tablet around the room, and Blair watched each man scrawl a signature. She rubbed the drive between her fingers as the tablet got closer to her. On second thought, maybe this was a mistake. She hesitated when the tablet got to her.

"Dr. Winters?" Carson asked from his seat. "Something wrong?"

"No, I just…"

SALVAGED VOWS

"Sign the damn tablet," Tanner muttered under his breath, earning a glare from both Carson and Benedict.

"You wouldn't be so quick to sign if it were the most important thing in your life," she shot back, adding her glare to the mix.

Tanner merely grunted, rolling his eyes and crossing his enormous arms over his chest. He sank back in his chair, his attention still heavy on her.

When she finally signed her signature after reading the few quick sentences Benedict had written, it felt as though her stomach was a churning whirlpool. Why did she feel like she was going to be sick?

"Here," she muttered, holding out the drive.

Penn reached for it, but Tanner intercepted it with surprising speed for a man his size. His fingers brushed Blair's, and she yanked her hand back.

"I'll handle security protocols for this data," he said, his voice lower than before.

Blair fought the urge to rub her fingers where his had touched. What the hell was that?

"I need your word this stays protected," she managed, hoping her voice sounded steadier than it felt.

"Mr. Whitney's security measures are... comprehensive," Carson assured her. "Now, we should discuss immediate protective measures for you personally."

Benedict nodded. "The whistleblower report includes your home address. Not safe to return there."

She hadn't even noticed, too concerned about what it meant for her research.

Fear, which Blair had been holding at bay with anger and pure determination, finally broke through. "You think I'm in physical danger?"

Before Carson could answer, Tanner spoke again, his voice flat and certain. "Yes."

"Oh," she murmured, rubbing the end of her sleeve again. "I...I guess I could find somewhere else to stay for a while. Maybe a hotel."

9

This wasn't just about her research or reputation. Someone wanted what she had badly enough to destroy her for it.

"It'll be safer if we take you to a secure location. I'll have Ms. Briggs, our head of security, look into it immediately," Carson said.

"What exactly does this all mean?" she asked.

Carson glanced at Tanner, a silent communication passing between them. Tanner gave an almost imperceptible nod.

"Since this is a high-profile case, Tanner will be personally responsible for your security," Carson said. "24/7 protection until this situation resolves."

Blair's gaze darted to Tanner, who watched her with the same unreadable expression. The thought of this intense, silent man shadowing her every move made something flutter uncomfortably in her stomach. It'd be like having the world's most imposing shadow following her around.

"I talk a lot," she blurted out. "Like, constantly. Everyone says so. I process verbally. It's how I think."

If she expected this warning to deter him, Tanner's response disappointed. He simply nodded once. "Noted."

"We need your decision, Dr. Winters," Carson pressed. "Are you engaging our services?"

Blair looked at Tanner again. His eyes held no warmth, no reassurance.

But what else was she supposed to do?

"Yes. I suppose I don't have any other choice."

"Excellent," Carson said, signaling the end of the meeting. "Once Ms. Briggs has determined a safe location, Tanner will escort you there and brief you on protocols."

As everyone rose, Blair battled against rising panic. In twenty-four hours, she'd lost her lab, her reputation, and now, apparently, her freedom of movement. Everything was spiraling beyond her control, like a chemical reaction.

Tanner stepped beside her, and she had to tilt her head back to look up at him. Damn, he was even more imposing standing. "You can wait in the main lobby until I come to get you." He left without another word.

"Great," she muttered under her breath. "Just fucking great."

CHAPTER TWO

TANNER

Tanner Whitney's headache started the moment Blair Winters opened her mouth in the conference room, and two hours later, it still hadn't stopped.

"I packed light, you know, but I need my research notebooks. They're not digitized. Old habit. I've always believed in keeping analog backups since that time in grad school when—"

Tanner tuned out her voice as he scanned the garage level of Crest Strategies. He cataloged exit points, potential cover positions, and blind spots; all while the scientist continued her verbal marathon. Two security cameras with overlapping blind spots near the south exit. Concrete pillars offering cover at thirty-foot intervals. Maintenance door requiring keycard access; potential extraction route if primary exits were compromised. The woman hadn't paused for breath once.

She was still going. "—and of course my medication. Not that I'm on anything serious. Just allergy pills. Connecticut pollen, you know? Though Manhattan's probably worse with all the—"

"Dr. Winters." He cut her off, keeping his voice low. "Silence until we reach the vehicle."

She blinked at him, her mouth closing and then immediately opening again. "But there's no one even here—"

"Security protocol." A lie, but an effective one. "Assume we're under surveillance."

That finally shut her up, though her expression suggested she had about forty-eight things she wanted to say. At least she followed instructions, a small mercy.

Tanner directed her toward one of the company's unmarked SUVs with his hand hovering near the small of her back but not touching her. The urge to make contact, to establish physical control of his asset, was purely tactical, he told himself. That his palm actually itched with the impulse was simply a complication.

He'd read her file that morning. Brilliant neurobiologist, breakthrough research, messy divorce years ago, lives alone. High-value target with minimal security awareness. A professional nightmare.

And Carson had mentioned taking drastic measures because of the potential her case could bring to Crest Strategies.

The thought made his jaw clench as he opened the SUV's passenger door. Blair slid in, her emerald blouse catching the fluorescent garage lighting. She smelled like the faint scent of vanilla and something chemical; lab sanitizer, probably. Tanner's senses cataloged the information automatically, along with the soft rustle of fabric as she settled into the seat. Irrelevant details. He filed them away.

He closed the door firmly and circled to the driver's side, giving himself exactly five seconds of mental reset before entering.

Five. The curve of her nose was objectively aesthetically proportioned. Four. The intensity in her eyes when discussing her research suggested intelligence that was genuinely impressive, if inconveniently packaged. Three. The threat to her was legitimate. Two. This was a standard protection assignment. One. Nothing more.

He slid behind the wheel and started the engine without a word. In his peripheral vision, Blair fidgeted with the strap of her bag, clearly uncomfortable with the silence.

Good. Silence was safer.

The SUV pulled out of the garage and merged into Manhattan traffic. Tanner kept his attention shifting—mirrors, blind spots, surrounding vehicles—while his mind processed the outrageous situation.

Blair lasted exactly two minutes and seventeen seconds before breaking.

"So where are we going? A safe house? Hotel? Secret underground bunker?" She gave a nervous laugh.

"Secure location."

"That's... not actually an answer."

"All you need to know."

She shifted in her seat. "Do you always speak in fragments?"

"When possible."

Blair sighed and bit her cheek. "Look, I understand the whole strong, silent protector thing you've got going on, but I've had a day from fucking hell. My life's work has been weaponized against me, my reputation is in tatters, and I'm currently in a car with a man who communicates exclusively in monosyllables. A little information would make this less traumatic."

Tanner glanced at her briefly. The genuine distress beneath her irritation was clear. Not his problem. Emotional comfort wasn't in his job description.

But operational clarity was.

"Midtown safe apartment," he conceded. "Temporarily. Until permanent arrangements are made."

Her shoulders relaxed. "Thank you. Was that so hard?"

He didn't answer, focusing instead on the black sedan that had been three cars back for the last ten blocks. Probably nothing, but he adjusted his route to be certain.

Blair had already moved on. "I'm guessing you're military, right? Former? The way you move, the situational awareness. Special Forces, I'm guessing."

Tanner kept his expression neutral. Her observation skills were better than he'd expected.

"Private contractor," he corrected, offering nothing more.

"Which means black ops stuff you can't talk about." She nodded as if she'd solved a puzzle. "Don't worry, I've worked with military types before. Research grants from DARPA and all that."

That caught his attention. "DARPA funding wasn't in your file."

"My ex"—her voice dropped, and she squirmed in her seat—" anyway, it was early in my career. Neural interface project. Didn't pan out, but I learned a lot about security clearances and classified protocols." She shrugged. "Also learned I prefer civilian research. Fewer strings. And guns."

"Your current research. Anyone else know it in entirety?"

"No one. I'm the only one with the full picture and formula. My team each had pieces, synthesis, testing, analysis, but I kept the complete structure to myself."

Smart. Compartmentalization reduced vulnerability.

"Is it replicable from the data you provided?"

Blair hesitated. "Theoretically. But there are elements that aren't documented. Intuitive adjustments I make during development."

So, the thumb drive wasn't a complete liability. Another fact to report to Carson.

They rode in silence for several blocks. Tanner confirmed they weren't being followed before taking an indirect route to the safe apartment. Blair seemed to have momentarily exhausted her need to fill the silence, instead watching the city through her window, her fingers tapping a restless rhythm on her thigh. She'd incessantly rubbed the sleeve of her shirt in the meeting. She may have been a genius, but she was not good at hiding her emotions or keeping her body language subtle.

She was easier to read than a picture book.

His phone vibrated once. Carson. The message was brief.

> Meeting. 8PM. Office.

Which meant Carson had decided. Tanner's jaw tightened. He already knew what the decision would be.

Fuck.

The safe apartment was on the 18th floor of an upscale building with private security and no shared ventilation systems. Tanner did a sweep while Blair stood in the entryway, exhaustion showing in the slump of her shoulders.

"Bedroom's through there," he said, emerging from the hallway. "Bathroom's stocked with essentials. The kitchen has basic supplies."

Blair nodded, taking in the sparsely furnished space. "And you'll be...?"

"Adjacent unit. Connected by a security door." He gestured to a heavy door beside the kitchen that looked like a closet but connected to the neighboring apartment. "Locked on both sides. Emergency access only."

"So I'll have privacy?"

"Limited. Apartment is monitored. Standard security protocol."

Her eyes widened. "Monitored? As in cameras?"

"Audio only. Living areas only." He'd expected this objection. "Non-negotiable."

Blair ran a hand through her blonde curls and wrinkled her nose. "That's invasive."

"Yeah. So is a fucking bullet," Tanner replied in a flat voice.

Something shifted in her expression, and she glanced over her shoulder at the windows, which were covered at the moment. She bit her lip again, her brow creasing. Good. Fear was appropriate. Fear bred caution. The slight tremor in her lower lip, however, triggered an unwelcome response in his chest; a tightening he immediately identified and suppressed. Emotional vulnerability was a liability, both hers and, more problematically, his own.

"How long will I be here?" She asked, her voice smaller than before.

"Unknown." He checked his watch. "I need to return to the office. The security system is active. Door locks automatically. Don't leave."

"What about clothes? Personal items?"

"Being handled." By whom he didn't specify because he didn't know and didn't care. "Delivery expected within two hours."

Blair crossed her arms. "And food? I haven't eaten since breakfast."

"Check the kitchen." He crossed his arms, jutting his chin towards the fridge. "If you find nothing there, delivery options are programmed into the tablet. Use the secure account." He moved toward the door. "Questions?"

Blair looked like she had about a hundred, but she only asked one. "When will you be back?"

Why would his return matter to her?

"When necessary," he answered, opening the door. "The system will alert me of any security concerns."

"That's not what I—" She stopped herself. "Never mind."

Tanner paused. Technically, he was abandoning a traumatized civilian in an unfamiliar environment. Operationally unsound.

"Two hours," he amended. "I'll return in two hours."

The immediate relief on her face was irritating. He was not responsible for her emotional comfort. He shouldn't be training her to rely on him for that.

But fuck.

He was responsible for her safety. And emotional stability affected compliance with security protocols.

That's all it was. Operational necessity.

———

"Abso-fucking-lutely not." Tanner stood rigid before Carson's desk, arms crossed. "Find another fucking solution."

Carson remained seated, fingertips pressed together, infuriatingly calm. It was moments like these that Tanner almost missed being in the military. At least the men who'd been in charge of him weren't arrogant prats. At least, not to Carson's level. "I've considered all options. This is the most effective approach."

"No, it's fucking not. It's unnecessary and excessive."

"It's neither. The legal protections of marriage provide coverage we can't otherwise secure."

James, leaning against the window, cleared his throat. "Tanner, spousal privilege alone solves multiple security issues. Anything she tells you becomes protected communication. They can't force you to testify against each other."

"You weren't here for the meeting, so you stay the fuck out of this," Tanner spat. "Besides, we're not facing criminal charges."

"Yet." Carson's voice hardened. "Her research has military applications, regardless of her intentions. If someone wants to frame her as a bioterrorist, they'll find a way. When that happens, I want every legal protection in place."

Tanner paced the length of the office, fighting the urge to put his fist through something. "There are other ways to secure her research. Physical protection, digital security, legal countermeasures."

"All of which we're already implementing," Carson said. "The marriage creates an additional layer of protection through marital property laws. If her assets are seized—including research—half technically belongs to you. And to us."

And there it was. The real reason.

"This isn't about protecting her," Tanner said, stopping to face Carson. "It's about controlling her research."

Carson didn't flinch. "It's about both. We protect what we control, and we control what we protect."

"You're doing the same thing to her that the other companies trying to acquire her research are doing, but in a shittier way."

"Yes, and no. We are genuinely trying to protect her and her assets. But I also believe she's a genius and her work is important. If it helps you sleep better at night, you could consider this as an investing opportunity."

"Then you fucking marry her."

Carson chuckled. "I think my fiancée might have something to say about that."

"Then make that asshole do it," Tanner growled, pointing to James. "Or Penn. Or the fucking president. I'm not getting fucking married. Especially not to some whiny scientist who doesn't shut up. Fuck no. I'm not doing it. Find someone else." Tanner's voice was steel.

"You are the best option." Carson stood, matching Tanner's stance, though Tanner had several inches on him. "You have the background to understand her research. You have the security clearance to inter-face with defense agencies. And you have no family entanglements that could complicate the arrangement."

"I'm not husband material."

"That's precisely why you're perfect for this." Carson's lips curved in a humorless smile. "This isn't about compatibility. It's about creating a legal and physical shield around Dr. Winters and her intel-lectual property."

"Have you considered her?" Tanner's jaw clenched. "She won't agree to it. Her file says she is divorced. I doubt she'll enter a marriage with a stranger, let alone me."

"She doesn't have a choice." Carson walked around the desk. "Nei-ther do you."

The temperature in the room seemed to drop ten degrees. Tanner's voice was dangerously quiet. "Meaning?"

"Meaning," Carson continued, unperturbed, "that Winters Biomedical's survival depends on our intervention. And your continued position with Crest Strategies depends on your cooperation with our strategy."

James pushed away from the window. "Carson—"

Carson raised a hand, silencing him. "I don't make this demand lightly, Tanner. But the situation requires extraordinary measures."

Tanner stared at his boss, at his friend. The man who'd recruited him four years ago when he'd been at his lowest, who'd given him purpose and direction when his military career imploded. Who had helped him work up to his first million, then his first billion. After Kandahar, Tanner hadn't expected a second chance; hadn't wanted one. Carson had offered it anyway, understanding that some lines wouldn't be crossed. Personal entanglement had been the first line on that list.

"Why are you threatening me?"

"It's not a threat, Tanner."

"What aren't you telling me, then?" Tanner asked.

Carson and James exchanged glances.

"Penn found something," James said. "The attack on Dr. Winters didn't originate with pharmaceutical competitors. It came from within the defense sector."

"Someone with high-level connections," Carson added. "Someone who can make people and research disappear into classified black holes."

"Military acquisition. Bypass the patents, classify the research, control development."

"Exactly," Carson nodded. "And Dr. Winters would likely face indefinite detention as a 'person of interest' while they strip-mine her brain for everything she knows."

The scenario was too familiar. A bright youthful face of a woman flashed in the back of Tanner's mind. A face that looked too similar to Tanner's own. A brilliant mind vanishing into government facilities, emerging years later as a hollow shell. At least she'd gotten out. Others didn't. Tanner couldn't save them all. He hadn't even been able to save her.

He turned away from Carson and James, facing the opposite wall where he forced himself to take a deep breath before he let emotions that didn't belong on his face slip through his defenses.

"She's not just facing professional ruin. You're saying they'll take her like they did Annabelle."

"Yes." Carson's voice was soft.

It was the vanishing act that ended with redacted files and closed-casket funerals, if there was a funeral at all.

"The marriage creates complications for them," James explained. "Legal entanglements. Public scrutiny. Harder to make a married woman disappear than a single female scientist with limited connections."

Tanner walked to the window, staring out at the darkening city. They were right about the strategic value. A marriage of convenience would create bureaucratic barriers that might buy enough time to neutralize the threat.

But the personal cost...

"Two conditions," he said finally, still facing the window. "First, it's temporary. Once the threat is gone, we get an immediate annulment."

"Agreed," Carson said without hesitation.

"Second, I maintain operational autonomy. No interference in my security protocols."

"Within reason."

Tanner turned. "No. Complete autonomy. Or find yourself another husband."

Carson studied him, then nodded once. "Granted. Anything else?"

There should have been. A hundred other conditions and contingencies. But right now, Tanner just wanted out of Carson's office, away from the trap he'd just agreed to walk into.

"When?" he asked.

"Three days," Carson replied. "Penn's working on documentation, creating a relationship history."

"I'm handling the legal framework," James added.

Three days to prepare for a marriage he didn't want to a woman who wouldn't stop talking.

But if he could stop this before it was Annabelle all over again...

"I'll inform Dr. Winters tomorrow," Carson added. "After she's had time to rest."

"No, I'll tell her." Tanner's response was immediate.

Carson raised an eyebrow. "You sure that's wise? Your people skills are somewhat—"

"My mission, my briefing." Tanner moved toward the door. "I'll handle it."

He left before Carson could object, striding down the corridor toward the elevator.

Marriage. The word itself felt like a landmine waiting to detonate. Some men weren't built for attachments. Some men destroyed what they touched. Carson knew this about him. Knew exactly why Tanner worked alone. Yet he was forcing his hand anyway.

What a great fucking friend.

The elevator doors closed, and Tanner allowed himself ten seconds of pure, unfiltered rage. Ten seconds to acknowledge the fury coursing through him. Ten seconds of weakness before he locked it away.

Ten. This compromised his operational independence. Nine. A

civilian attachment created vulnerability. Eight. Her constant talking would drive him insane. Seven. Those intelligent hazel eyes would see too much. Six. She would expect emotional engagement. Five. He would fail at this, as he had failed at it before. Four. Irrelevant. This was a mission, not a relationship. Three. The aim was protection, not connection. Two. He would adapt and overcome. As always. One. She would never know what this cost him, and she would never know that he was doing this for Annabelle. For his little sister.

Tanner's expression remained carved from stone, his body language revealing nothing of the silent profanities cycling through his mind. To anyone watching, he was simply a professional accepting an assignment. Only he knew that behind his impassive facade, he was calculating exactly how many ways this forced marriage would destroy the barricades he'd built around himself.

He had a ring to get and a proposal to plan. A chain to forge, linking him to a woman whose very breathing pattern grated against his nerves.

God help them both.

CHAPTER THREE

BLAIR

FOUR HOURS OF FITFUL SLEEP HAD DONE LITTLE TO restore Blair's equilibrium after yesterday's cascade of disasters. Her lab seized, reputation destroyed, and now this sterile safe house that felt more like a cage than protection.

"Status assessment," she continued, the sound of her own voice oddly comforting in the empty apartment. "Assets: brain still functioning. One thumb drive of research being guarded by six-foot-six of tactical silence. Crest Strategies is presumably working on reputation rehabilitation." She reached for the toothbrush someone had thoughtfully provided. "Liabilities: literally everything else."

Blair wrapped herself in the provided robe, surprisingly soft against her skin, and padded to the kitchen. The coffee maker beckoned, the one reliable constant in a world suddenly devoid of certainty.

"Coffee. Then recalibrate. Then—"

Three sharp knocks at the door made her jump. Before she could respond, the lock disengaged with a soft click.

Of course. Locks were apparently optional concepts to her guard dog.

He filled the doorway with his imposing frame, a paper bag in one hand and storm clouds in his eyes. His gaze swept over her. She knew what he saw: the robe, bare legs, disheveled curls. It was what any straight man would notice. His attention snapped back to her face. Yeah. His mind was definitely where she thought it was.

"You're awake," he said, as if this required confirmation.

"Observational skills like that must be why they pay you the big bucks," Blair replied. She resisted the urge to tug the robe lower. "I'd have appreciated a chance to get dressed before you barged in."

"Brought breakfast." He held up the paper bag. "Get dressed. We need to talk."

"Fine. Five minutes." She grabbed the clothes that had been delivered last night and retreated to the bathroom.

While dressing, Blair's mind churned through possibilities, anxiety manifesting as an internal monologue that would soon become external. What fresh hell awaited her today? Had they found something sinister in her research? Was her lab being completely dismantled? Were criminal charges being filed?

By the time she emerged, her nervous energy had crystallized into verbal momentum.

"If this is about the neural binding protocols in section four of my research, I can explain the molecular similarities to synthetic neurotoxins. It's a classic case of structural homology without functional equivalence. The science board clearly didn't understand the protein markers that inhibit systemic spread beyond damaged tissue. I tried to explain, but they had clearly made up their minds before I even—"

"Sit down," Tanner interrupted, gesturing to the small dining table where he'd arranged breakfast: bagels, cream cheese, fruit, and coffee.

Blair blinked, thrown off by both the interruption and the surprisingly thoughtful spread. "You brought actual food."

"People need to eat." He pulled out a chair. "Sit."

She sat, watching as he took the seat across from her. He hadn't touched the food, just watched her with that steady, assessing gaze that made her feel like a specimen under a microscope. He filled the small kitchen space. Not just physically with his broad shoulders and imposing height, but somehow energetically, as if the very air

24

contracted around him. She simultaneously wanted to step back and, irrationally, to move closer. Strange.

"Eat," he said, pushing a plate toward her.

"Are you going to use actual sentences today, or are we sticking with one-word commands?" She reached for a bagel despite herself. "Because I have to say, the caveman communication style isn't—"

"We need to get married."

Blair's hand froze halfway to her mouth, bagel suspended in midair. Her brain, usually racing ahead with multiple thought tracks, stuttered to a complete halt.

"I—what?" She set the bagel down, certain she'd misheard. "Sorry, did you just say married? As in, to each other? As in, legally binding matrimony? As in—"

"Yes." Tanner's expression hadn't changed, but something in his shoulders had tightened. "Security measure. It's legal protection for you and your research."

Blair stared at him, waiting for the punchline. When none came, she erupted into nervous laughter.

"That's—that's absurd. I mean, completely insane. We just met yesterday. I don't even know your middle name. Or your birthday. Or if you have any hobbies besides terrifying people with your silence. Marriage is—it's not a security protocol, it's a relationship, a partnership. It's—"

"It's a legal designation that provides specific protections," Tanner cut in. "Spousal privilege means they can't force either of us to testify against the other. Joint property laws protect your research assets from seizure. Family medical rights ensure access if you're detained or hospitalized."

Blair's analytical mind kicked in despite her emotional whiplash, analyzing his points. The logic was sound. Marriage would create legal barriers between her research and whoever wanted to steal it.

"This is Mr. Crest's idea," she said, not a question.

Tanner nodded once. She caught a flash of something in his eyes when Carson's name was mentioned; not just resistance but something deeper, almost primal. The muscle in his jaw ticked once, twice, his hands momentarily curling into fists before relaxing. Whatever Tanner Whitney had been before this, he was clearly a man accustomed to containing volatile elements within himself. He at least had that, plus six inches, over her ex-husband.

"And you're... what? Just following orders? Volunteering for spouse duty?" She pushed away from the table, needing to move. "This is ridiculous. There have to be other options."

"There aren't." His voice remained level, matter-of-fact, but the tension in his shoulders told a different story. "Not with the time constraints and threat level."

"Threat level?" Blair stopped pacing. "What exactly aren't you telling me? What threat level?"

Tanner planted his feet shoulder-distance apart. "The attack came from within the defense sector. High-level connections. People who can make problems disappear."

"You mean people who can make *me* disappear."

Tanner didn't soften the blow. "Yes."

"Shit." She pressed a trembling hand to her forehead. "Shit!" Blair resumed pacing, arms wrapped around herself. "So marriage to you creates what? Bureaucratic paperwork that makes it harder for them to black-bag me in the night? How long would that actually stop them if they really wanted me?"

"Long enough to identify and neutralize the threat."

"And then what? We just... get divorced? 'Thanks for the temporary protection. Have a pleasant life'?"

"Annulment," he corrected. "Pre-arranged. Clean break once the threat is eliminated."

"This isn't just some guy who wants to kidnap me. If it really is related to the defense sector, you're talking about the fucking government. You can't just glare at them and expect them to go away. This is... This is..." She couldn't find the right word for the shitstorm it was.

Tanner just watched her spiral.

"I was married before, but you probably already knew that." She glanced at him, and he shrugged. Of course he did. "It didn't end well.

He was... Well, for starters, he said I talked too much, thought too much, worked too much. That I was more married to my research than to him. To be fair, that was because working with potentially dangerous substances was better than being around some who couldn't control his... Never mind. The point is, marriage sucks. I know that firsthand." She laughed without humor. "It's ironic that now my research is the reason I'd be getting married again." She paused in the middle of her pacing and faced him. "What about you? Don't you have a girlfriend who would oppose your getting married to a complete stranger? Don't you have any personal objections to this? Or do you just accept whatever mission gets assigned to you without question?"

His eyes darkened, pupils dilating. "According to Carson, my preferences are irrelevant."

"Your preferences—" Blair threw up her hands. "We're talking about marriage! Legal, binding marriage! How is that irrelevant?"

"Because the alternative is worse." Tanner finally stood, his height and presence suddenly filling the small kitchen. The motion brought him closer to her, close enough that she could detect the faint scent of something distinctly masculine that made her pulse quicken against her will. "Without protection, they will take you. They've done it before to others, and they will do it again. They will take your research. They will extract everything you know through whatever means necessary. Then they will make you disappear."

"You sound like you've seen it happen."

"I have." Something haunted flickered behind his eyes, there and gone so quickly Blair almost missed it.

She sat back down, legs suddenly unsteady. "When would this happen? This marriage."

"Two days from now. Documentation is being prepared. Small ceremony, minimal witnesses."

"Two days?" Her voice rose an octave. "As in two days from today? As in, I don't even get seventy-two hours to process the fact that I'm marrying a man I met yesterday? A man who, by the way, clearly considers this entire arrangement about as pleasant as a root canal?"

Tanner didn't bother denying it. The slight tightening around his eyes told her everything she needed to know about his personal feelings about their impending union.

"Time is critical," he said, turning away. In profile, the hard line of his jaw appeared carved from granite.

She pressed her palms against her eyes and then held out her arm towards him. "Pinch me."

"What the fuck?"

"Pinch me."

"Why?"

"Yesterday I was a respected scientist. Now I'm considering marrying a stranger to avoid being disappeared by shadowy government operatives. I think I'm having a nightmare. Maybe something happened in the lab and I'm in a coma. Maybe—Ow!"

He pinched her.

"Fuck, Tanner, that hurt."

"You asked," Tanner said, checking his watch. "I need an answer about the marriage within the hour."

Blair rubbed her arm where he'd honored her request. "Is it really my decision, though? You've made it abundantly clear that my options are marry you or potentially disappear forever. That's not a choice. That's coercion."

"Yes. But the consent must be yours."

She studied him, this hard, silent man who might become her husband within the week's end. His expression revealed nothing.

"If, and I mean if, I agreed to this insanity, I would need conditions," Blair said, scientist brain activating again despite emotional turmoil. "Parameters. Boundaries."

Tanner nodded once. "That's reasonable."

"Condition one: My research remains mine. Anything developed during or after this... arrangement remains my intellectual property."

"Agreed."

"Condition two: this is a professional arrangement only. No..." she gestured vaguely between them, heat rising in her cheeks, "expectations."

Something that might have been amusement flickered in his eyes, along with something darker that made her stomach flip. "Agreed."

"Condition three: I maintain autonomy in all areas not directly related to security. My work, my schedule, my communication with colleagues once cleared by your team."

He considered this one longer. "Restricted autonomy. The security protocols supersede when necessary."

Blair opened her mouth to argue, then closed it. His terms were actually reasonable given the circumstances.

"Fine. Condition four: When this is over, we get that annulment immediately. No delays, no complications."

"Already arranged. The documentation is being prepared with the marriage certificate."

Of course it was. He'd been ten steps ahead throughout the entire conversation.

Blair took a deep breath, trying to calm her racing heart. "One last question. Why you? Specifically? Surely Crest Strategies has other security personnel who could serve this function."

For the first time, Tanner seemed uncomfortable.

"Military background. Understanding of the defense sector. Security clearance levels. Specific qualifications." His clipped response revealed more in its brevity than a paragraph of explanation could have.

"In other words, you drew the short straw," Blair translated.

Tanner's jaw flexed once, a tiny crack in his façade. "Not my mission preference."

Rude, but okay. Fair enough.

Blair stood, needing to move again. "This is absolutely insane. I need. I need to think."

Tanner headed for the door. "I'll be next door."

When she was alone again, Blair resumed her pacing, talking through the problem aloud.

"What are my options? Agree to this marriage of convenience with Tall, Dark, and Dangerous, or risk disappearing into some black site where they extract my research through dubious means. Great. Option one certainly wins out there, unfortunately." She ran her hands through her hair. "What's the risk assessment, Blair? Well, the marriage is temporary, contractual, and provides actual legal protection. Temporary is good. And a refusal might lead to my inevitable permanent disappearance or worse. Just fucking peachy."

She stopped at the window, careful to stand to the side as Tanner had instructed the previous night before leaving. "Okay, what are the emotional variables? Well, my previous nightmare of a marriage created psychological resistance. And then there's Tanner's evident reluctance, which doesn't exactly inspire loads of confidence. God he hates me. And that would, of course, lead to a complete lack of a genuine relationship foundation."

A new thought occurred to her, one she was reluctant to voice even to herself. The inexplicable physical awareness she felt in Tanner's presence; the way her pulse quickened when he stood too close; the heat that pooled low in her belly when his voice dropped to that dangerous register.

Fuck, she hadn't experienced that since before her marriage to the monster had ended.

"Stupid variable," she whispered. "Fucking unwanted physiological response to the subject. Shit. It requires further analysis, and it's potentially problematic."

Blair's reflection stared back at her from the glass, worried eyes in a pale face.

"But scientifically speaking," she continued, "the evidence unfortunately supports his proposed solution. It's a matter of temporary discomfort versus potential destruction. And that means my logical choice is clear, regardless of emotional or... physiological objections."

She thought of her research, years of work that could help thousands of patients with spinal injuries. Would she let it disappear because she was uncomfortable with a paper marriage?

Twenty-seven minutes later, Blair knocked on the connecting door between apartments. It opened immediately.

"Fine," she said without preamble. "I consent to this arrangement.

But I want everything in writing, all conditions, all parameters, all expectations."

Tanner studied her face, then nodded once. "Already done."

Of course it was.

———

Two days later, Blair stood in a private suite at Crest Strategies headquarters, surrounded by an unexpected flurry of wedding preparations she hadn't anticipated for a "security arrangement." A stylist fussed with her hair while a makeup artist hovered nearby with an array of products that seemed excessive for what was essentially a legal transaction.

"Is all this really necessary?" She asked Benedict, who coordinated the operation, tablet in hand as he checked off items from what appeared to be a detailed timeline. "I thought this was supposed to be a small, private ceremony."

"It is," Benedict replied, not looking up from his screen. "But appearances matter. The marriage needs to seem legitimate to outside observers."

"So I need to look like a blushing bride rather than a scientist being coerced into a security arrangement?" She couldn't keep the edge out of her voice.

That got his attention. He glanced up. "No one is being coerced, Dr. Winters. This is a mutual agreement for mutual benefit."

"Tell that to your colleague," Blair muttered, wincing as the stylist tugged at a stubborn curl. "He looks about as enthusiastic as someone facing a firing squad."

Benedict shook his head. "Tanner has his reasons. Don't take it personally."

"Hard not to take it personally when I'm about to legally bind myself to someone who can barely stand to be in the same room with me."

Benedict studied her for a moment. "It's not you he's resisting."

Before Blair could press for clarification, the stylist returned with the final dress selection, and the moment was lost.

The dress they'd selected was simple but elegant, a knee-length ivory sheath that Blair had to admit was flattering. Not a traditional wedding gown, but clearly special-occasion attire. Her hair was styled into a more polished version of her natural curls, and the makeup enhanced without masking.

"Not bad," she admitted to her reflection. "Though I still feel like I'm playing dress-up in someone else's life."

A knock at the door preceded Carson's entrance. He surveyed her with an approving nod.

"Dr. Winters. You look lovely."

"It's quite a production for a sham marriage," Blair replied, running her hands nervously down the sides of the dress.

Carson's smile never faltered. "There's no such thing as a sham marriage in legal terms. Only legal and illegal unions. Yours will be perfectly legal, I assure you."

"And perfectly temporary."

"As agreed." He offered his arm. "Shall we? The officiant is waiting."

Blair hesitated. "Where's Tanner? Shouldn't the groom be present for his own wedding?"

"Already in position. Security protocols."

Of course. Even his own wedding was an operation. Why had she expected anything different after two days of watching him approach everything as if it were a military campaign?

Blair took Carson's arm, allowing him to lead her to a small conference room that had been transformed. Flowers adorned the table that had been pushed against one wall to serve as an altar of sorts. A few chairs faced forward, occupied by Benedict, Penn (who seemed more interested in something on his tablet than the proceedings), and a man she'd been introduced to that morning, James Rothschild. He gave her a reassuring smile.

Tanner stood at the front in a charcoal suit that fit his broad shoulders perfectly, his tattooed forearms covered for once by crisp shirt sleeves. His expression was, of course, stone.

Great.

His gaze met hers as she entered, and something flickered there. For a heartbeat, his gaze lingered on her in a way that wasn't entirely professional, trailing from her face down the contours of her dress before snapping back to attention.

The officiant, a justice of the peace who appeared completely unruffled by the unusual circumstances, smiled as Carson led Blair to stand beside Tanner.

"Ready?" the officiant asked.

Blair fought the urge to laugh hysterically. Ready? To marry a stranger under duress to avoid government kidnapping? Sure, she'd been preparing for this her whole life.

"Yes," she said instead, her voice surprisingly steady.

The ceremony was brief. The standard vows were replaced with simplified promises of partnership and respect; no love, no cherishing, just practical commitments appropriate to their arrangement. Blair spoke her parts automatically. The scientific part of her mind observed the process with detached fascination while the emotional parts of her mind remained in stunned disbelief, quietly murmuring swear words that tickled her brain.

And then came the rings. She hadn't expected rings.

Tanner produced two simple platinum bands from his pocket. The weight of the metal felt strange as he slid the smaller band onto her finger, his calloused hand briefly engulfing hers. The contact lasted less than a second.

When it was her turn, she had to reach up to complete the exchange, her smaller fingers brushing against his as she slid the ring into place. For the briefest moment, their gazes met, and the heat she found there left her momentarily breathless. Then, just like that, the bulletproof shields he kept as a mask slammed back into place.

"By the power vested in me by the State of New York, I now pronounce you husband and wife."

No instructions to kiss the bride, thank god. Blair wasn't sure she could have maintained her composure through that formality, especially with her mind suddenly wandering to places it had no business going.

Just like that, it was done. Blair Winters had become Blair Whitney. On paper, at least.

The small group offered perfunctory congratulations. Penn finally looked up from his tablet long enough to nod in their general direction before returning to whatever had captured his attention. Benedict shook Tanner's hand. James remained professionally neutral as he patted Tanner on the back and earned a glare from her husband.

Shit.

Her husband.

What the fuck had she just agreed to?

Carson signed something on the tablet the officiant presented. "All legal documentation is complete. Your marriage certificate will be filed immediately. The, ah, other document we discussed remains in escrow until the appropriate time."

The annulment papers. Already prepared, already waiting in the wings for this temporary arrangement to end. That, at least, was a relief.

Not that she wanted two failed marriages under her belt. But the sooner, she supposed, the better.

"Security transport is ready. We should move now to maintain the timeline," Tanner said, lifting his chin. His hand settled at the small of her back, not quite touching but close enough to guide her movement. The proximity sent a rush of warmth through her that was as unwelcome as it was unexpected.

"Time to go."

Blair had so many questions, so many concerns, but the words tangled in her throat. Instead, she simply nodded and allowed herself to be escorted from the room, a bride with no celebration, no joy, no certainty of anything except the legal shield her new status provided.

The ride back to the safe apartment passed in silence. She couldn't bring herself to process verbally. Blair watched the city through tinted windows. Three days ago, she'd been a respected scientist. Now she was a security risk with a new husband she barely knew, who communicated primarily in grunts and glares.

"So," she finally said as they rode the elevator up to the 18th floor, unable to bear the silence any longer, "should I change my email signature, or is that too committed for a marriage with a pre-planned expiration date?"

Tanner didn't even glance at her. "Your choice."

"Helpful as always," she muttered.

The elevator doors opened, and they walked to the apartment door. Tanner unlocked it, then stepped aside to let her enter first.

The space looked exactly as they'd left it that morning. Somehow, that was annoying, as if the world couldn't be bothered to acknowledge the shitshow her life had become.

"I need to establish parameters," Blair said, turning to face him as he closed the door. "Ground rules. Expectations. I can't function in undefined circumstances."

Tanner nodded once. "Okay."

"Right. So." She began pacing, organizing her thoughts aloud. "Sleeping arrangements. I assume we maintain separate quarters as discussed."

"Correct."

"Daily routines. I need lab access as soon as possible. My research can't stall indefinitely."

"Being arranged."

"Personal space. We both need it. I process verbally. You... don't. How do we make that work in shared quarters?"

For the first time, Tanner seemed to consider her question seriously. "Designated zones. Times. Parameters that allow for both requirements."

Blair nodded, relieved he was actually engaging. "Good. That's... workable."

"In addition to...this," he said, gesturing between the two of them. "Carson has added some other items we have to fulfill."

Her stomach dropped. "What kinds of items? I thought we were going to get an annulment. I will not sleep with you, if that's what you're—"

"Fuck no." Tanner shook his head. "Public appearances. Limited but necessary. Marriage must appear legitimate."

"Oh, thank goodness." She paused and then frowned. "Wait, you mean we'll have to pretend to be an actual couple? In public?"

"Limited contact. Nothing excessive."

She was still trying to conceal her body's ridiculous thought to the mere potential idea of physical contact between them. She silently cursed her body's irrational response to the man.

"Right. Of course." Blair wrapped her arms around herself, suddenly chilled despite the apartment's comfortable temperature. "Don't you find any of this strange?" she pressed. "Or are you just that detached from normal human reactions?"

"My reactions are irrelevant to a mission's success."

"There! That!" Blair threw up her hands. "This isn't a mission. It's a marriage. Legally binding. We're now officially each other's next of kin. Doesn't that register at all on your emotional radar?"

"No."

"I don't believe you," she said, stepping closer. "No one is that emotionally disconnected. Not even special ops soldiers with thousand-yard stares and monosyllabic vocabularies."

Tanner's jaw tightened. "Believe what you want."

"Oh, I intend to." She moved still closer, entering his personal space deliberately. "And I think underneath all that tactical stoicism is a man who's just as uncomfortable with this situation as I am. The difference is, I'm honest about it."

For a long moment, they stood facing each other. Blair waited for him to step back, to re-establish the professional distance he'd maintained since they met.

Instead, Tanner leaned forward, his voice dropping to a register that sent a shiver down her spine.

"You want honesty, Dr. Winters? Here it is. This arrangement is tactically sound but personally problematic. You talk too much. You question everything. You push boundaries better left undisturbed."

His gaze locked with hers. "But none of that matters because my job is to keep you alive and your research secure, regardless of personal preferences. And right now, you're making that job harder."

"Well," she said, her voice not quite steady, "at least that was more than one syllable."

Something dangerous flashed in Tanner's eyes. He lifted his hand. She flinched.

Tanner's hand froze in mid-air. Blair's body had already tensed, shoulders hunching, arms lifting in a defensive posture she hadn't consciously chosen. The movement was automatic. Muscle memory from a different time, a different man.

His expression shifted, the hard lines softening into something she hadn't seen before. Surprise. Concern, even.

"I was going to fix my shirt," he spoke in a low voice. "I wasn't going to hit you."

Heat rushed to her face. Of course he wasn't. She knew that intellectually, but her body had reacted before her brain could process.

"I know that," she managed. The room felt suddenly too small. Her heart hammered against her ribs, and the edges of her vision darkened. Fucking great. She'd thought she'd gotten past this familiar onset of panic she thought she'd left behind years ago. Her therapist owed her a refund.

Blair took several steps back, needing distance, needing to breathe. "I should... it's been a long day. I'm going to get ready for bed."

The walls of the apartment seemed to close in. A few years of therapy, and still, a simple raised hand could catapult her back. Great. Just great.

"Dr. Winters—" Tanner started, a question in his voice.

"It's fine. I'm fine." The words tumbled out automatically. They were the same ones she'd offered to concerned colleagues when she'd shown up with sunglasses indoors. The same reassurances she'd given herself in the mirror while covering bruises with makeup. "Just tired. Wedding day and all that. You can let yourself out."

She attempted a smile that felt more like a grimace and retreated toward the bedroom. Her fight-or-flight response had no appropriate outlet.

The soft click of the door closing behind her released something in her chest. Blair leaned against it, sliding down until she sat on the floor, drawing her knees to her chest. Her breathing came in shallow gasps.

In. Out. Count to four. Hold. Release.

She was safe here. This man wasn't her ex-husband.

This marriage wasn't real.

But the fear... that was real enough.

CHAPTER FOUR

TANNER

THE PLATINUM BAND ON TANNER'S LEFT HAND BURNED. Not even twenty-four hours into the marriage, and he was already losing control of the operation.

Tanner braced his hands against the balcony railing, scanning the perimeter of the safe apartment while dawn broke over Manhattan. Six sniper positions on adjacent rooftops. Four access points requiring security overrides. Two emergency extraction routes. All cataloged, all insufficient to quiet the echo of Blair's flinch when he'd raised his hand last night.

That instinctive recoil had told him everything her words hadn't. Someone had trained that reaction into her body. A ghost he couldn't eliminate with firepower.

The thought made his molars grind.

His watch read 0615. Blair remained asleep in the adjacent apartment—not that he'd checked physically. The thermal imaging he'd installed after her reaction last night showed her heat signature still in bed, pulse rate indicating REM sleep. For security, he told himself. Not because he wanted to know if she thrashed from nightmares or cried when she thought no one could see.

Tanner's phone vibrated against his thigh. Carson.

> Reputation rehabilitation strategy meeting at 1100. Both of you required.

He sent back a single word.

Confirmed.

Taking one final sweep of sight lines and potential infiltration points, Tanner stepped back inside, shutting the balcony door. The coffee maker hummed to life on schedule—0620, like every morning since his discharge from Special Forces. Some routines survived even when everything else went to shit.

The connecting door between the apartments remained closed. After she'd retreated to her bedroom last night, trembling from a trauma response he recognized too well, he'd given her space. Relocated to the adjacent unit as planned. Kept his distance physically while monitoring remotely.

But everything felt wrong—the operational parameters, the artificial marriage, his own disturbing impulse to tear apart whoever had hurt her.

Tanner poured coffee into a mug, the rich bitterness scalding his tongue. Perfect. Pain sharpened focus. After a shower that cycled from scalding to freezing—another post-Kandahar habit—he changed into tactical pants and a button-down that concealed his shoulder holster.

He stood before the connecting door, weighing options. Protocol dictated a security check-in. The most efficient approach would be a text message.

His thumbs hovered over the screen:

> Good morning. Security check-in required.
> Meeting at Crest Strategies HQ at 1100.

He deleted it with a muttered "fuck this." A text was too impersonal. They were legally married. Supposedly living together. A text would establish a pattern of cold detachment that could undermine their cover.

The mission, he reminded himself. This was about the mission.

The sound of movement filtered through the wall. Cabinet doors opening, water running. She was awake. Tanner knocked on the connecting door, three precise raps that matched the cadence drilled into him during breach protocol training.

"Just a minute!" Her voice carried through the door, followed by rushing footsteps and what sounded like something being knocked over.

The door swung open to reveal Blair in an oversized MIT t-shirt and sleep shorts that showcased legs toned from what he guessed were hours pacing her lab. Her dark curls formed a chaotic halo around her face, eyes still heavy with sleep. She clutched a coffee mug in both hands like it contained liquid salvation rather than caffeine.

The dark circles beneath her eyes matched the bruise-purple of a dawn sky before a sandstorm. She hadn't slept well.

"Security check," he said, immediately recognizing the tactical error when her expression shuttered like blast doors closing.

"I'm alive, as you can see." She gestured to herself with her free hand, a nervous energy animating the movement. "Security status: exhausted but intact. No assassination attempts or government kidnappings to report."

She turned away, leaving the door open. Tanner recognized the reluctant invitation and followed her into the kitchen, maintaining distance. If their positions had been reversed, he'd have wanted space. But Blair was different. She filled silences, needing interaction. It was a foreign concept to him, but one he needed to accommodate for operational success.

For their marriage.

"We have a meeting at Crest Strategies. Eleven hundred hours," he said, watching as she refilled her coffee mug. The ceramic trembled slightly in her grip—caffeine overload or stress response. Both, probably.

"Translation for those of us who don't speak military?"

"Eleven AM."

"Right. Got it." She leaned against the counter, studying him over the rim of her mug. Steam fogged her glasses briefly, obscuring those sharp hazel eyes. "Sleep well in your separate apartment, husband?"

The word sounded strange coming from her lips, edged with something between sarcasm and genuine discomfort. His gaze dropped to those lips, lingering there until his situational awareness screamed warning.

"Adequately," he answered, then because it seemed necessary to return the inquiry, added, "You?"

"Oh, fantastically. Nothing helps me sleep like wondering if shadowy government operatives are planning to kidnap me while I try to process the fact that I'm legally married to a man who communicates primarily through grunts." She took another sip of coffee. The mug's slogan read "Sarcasm: Just One Of My Many Talents." Accurate. "So yes, just peachy."

The words tumbled out of her in that characteristic verbal spillage that simultaneously irritated and fascinated him. Her thought process was like watching an uncontrolled demolition; chaotic but following invisible patterns of structural collapse.

"We should establish protocols," he said, ignoring her sarcasm. "Daily routines. Expectations."

"Ironic that I suggested exactly that last night before..." She trailed off, breaking eye contact. Her fingers brushed the sleeve of her shirt unconsciously; self-soothing behavior he'd noted yesterday. "Anyway. Yes. Protocols. Good."

Tanner assessed the apartment. "The kitchen will be neutral territory. We should share meals when schedules permit."

Blair nodded. "What about a morning schedule? I heard you get up before the sun. I don't do that. I like sleep, even if it doesn't like me. Also, fair warning, I take forever in the morning. It takes about a gallon of coffee for me to be able to make a single coherent sentence."

"You must spend a lot of time in the bathroom."

She froze and stared at him with her mouth open. "Did you just make a joke?"

"Believe it or not, I am capable."

"Of course you are." A small smile played at the corners of her mouth, and his itched to copy it.

What the actual fuck? He didn't want to smile; this woman was just a master manipulator. That's what it was. And shit, she was talking again. Tanner forced his mind to focus on her question.

"What about... I mean, public appearances? As a couple? You mentioned Carson wanted us to do that."

"It'll be limited. Strategic. The first one is next week. Charity function." He watched her reaction closely. "Hand-holding. Minimal physical contact."

He noted the slight color that rose to her cheeks and filed it away. Irrelevant to the mission but impossible to ignore, like unexplained heat signatures on an otherwise clear thermal scan.

"Right. Professional affection. I can handle that." She set her mug down with a decisive click. "What about my research? I need to work. Sitting here waiting to be saved is driving me crazy."

"Your lab access is being arranged in a secure location. Limited personnel."

"When?"

"Three days. Pending final security protocols."

Blair's shoulders relaxed minutely, and Tanner recognized the relief for what it was. Her research wasn't just work. It was her identity; her purpose. Taking that away was like stripping a soldier of their weapon in hostile territory.

Something he understood better than she might expect.

"Thank you," she breathed. "I need... I need to feel useful. To keep moving forward."

The gratitude in her voice felt undeserved. He was simply executing operational parameters. But the warmth in her eyes triggered something uncomfortable in his chest, a pressure like the seconds after the pin is pulled but before the grenade detonates.

"I'll cook breakfast," he said abruptly, changing the subject.

"You cook?" Her eyebrows rose in genuine surprise.

"Basic field nutrition. Protein. Carbohydrates. Essential nutrients."

Blair laughed, the sound cutting through the tension like a combat knife through parachute cord. "That's not cooking; that's survival. Let me guess, military rations and protein shakes are your specialty?"

He didn't answer, moving to the refrigerator instead. But the corner of his mouth twitched, almost imperceptibly.

"Oh my god, I'm right!" She clapped her hands together, delight breaking across her face like sunrise after a night patrol. "The big, bad security specialist survives on MREs and protein powder. I bet you eat everything in precisely timed intervals for optimal performance."

"Efficient," he defended, pulling eggs and vegetables from the refrigerator.

"Depressing," she countered, moving beside him to peer at his selections. "Here, let me help. I actually enjoy cooking when I'm not buried in lab work."

Their hands brushed as she reached for the peppers he'd set on the counter. The contact lasted less than a second, but Tanner registered the softness of her skin, the slight tremor in her fingers, the way she quickly withdrew. Her proximity unleashed a cascade of sensory information: vanilla-scented shampoo, the faint rhythm of her pulse visible at her throat, the shape of her collarbone peeking from beneath her oversized shirt.

He stepped back. Tactical retreat.

"I'll handle your excessive amounts of coffee," he muttered, turning away from the neurochemical reaction her proximity triggered; elevated dopamine, accelerated heart rate, heightened sensory awareness. Combat readiness or attraction. The symptoms were disturbingly similar.

They worked in relative silence, the only sounds being the sizzle of vegetables in the pan and Blair's occasional humming; a melody he couldn't identify but that reminded him of long drives through Virginia countryside before his second deployment. It was oddly domestic, a simulation of normalcy in their decidedly abnormal arrangement.

When the food was ready, they sat at the small dining table, an island of forced domesticity in the sterile, safe apartment. The table had been positioned strategically—clear sight lines to all entry points, optimal distance from potential blast radius if the windows were breached, direct access to the concealed weapons cache beneath the floorboards.

"So," Blair said between bites, "when you're not playing reluctant husband to scientists in distress, what do you actually do at Crest Strategies?"

Tanner contemplated his response. "Security consultation. Threat assessment. Specialized intervention when necessary."

"Specialized intervention. That sounds ominous." She studied him, scientist's eyes dissecting his expressions for data points. "Is that how you ended up at Crest? Through your military connections?"

Tanner set down his fork. "Yes. After Kandahar."

"What happened in Kandahar?" Blair asked softly.

For a moment, he considered shutting down the line of questioning. It was his standard response to personal inquiries. But they were married now, however temporarily. Some level of disclosure might be strategically sound.

"Operation went wrong. Civilian casualties. I was extracted. Honorably discharged." The simplified version omitted the screaming children, the blood-soaked prayer rug, the night terrors that still occasionally shocked him awake at 0300 with the taste of Afghan dust in his mouth. "Twenty-seven civilian deaths. Eight children. Direct result of the intel I provided."

Blair's eyes widened slightly at the specificity, but she didn't recoil. "And Carson offered an alternative application for your skill set?"

"Yes. He found me at Arlington. Visiting graves." The men he'd lost because of his miscalculation. The weight of his failure etched into granite markers.

Blair seemed to sense there was more but didn't push. Instead, she offered something unexpected—her own vulnerability.

"My ex-husband was at DARPA. Defense contractor. We met when I was working on the neural interface project." She traced patterns on the table with her fingertip, precise geometric shapes that seemed to calm her. "I was young and naïve. He seemed so steady at first. Controlled. I found that attractive after dating academics who were all theory and no substance. He knew what he wanted in the world, and he took it. He was so confident. It looked attractive. Still probably would to the outside world."

Tanner remained silent, recognizing the importance of allowing her to continue at her own pace.

"Turns out that control extended to every aspect of our relationship. What I wore. Who I spoke to. How I conducted my research, among other more intimate things." Her voice remained steady, clinical almost, as if discussing tissue samples rather than personal trauma. "The criticism was subtle at first. I think that started even before I agreed to marry him. But soon enough, behind closed doors, it stopped being subtle; the gaslighting, the manipulations, the degradation..."

The muscles in Tanner's jaw flexed so hard he felt a tendon threaten to snap. "He hit you."

Not a question. He'd suspected as much since her reaction last night.

Blair's fingers stilled on the table. "Not at first. He was too smart for that. It started as psychological abuse—isolating me from colleagues, undermining my confidence, questioning my research methodology. By the time it turned physical, I was already convinced I deserved it." She gave a hollow laugh. "Three PhDs and I still couldn't see what was happening until it was too late."

Tanner's hand tightened around his coffee mug until the ceramic protested. Heat spread through his chest, a familiar rage seeking tactical application. The urge to find this nameless, faceless man and dismantle him piece by piece—starting with the hands he'd dared raise against her—felt visceral, immediate. Inappropriate. Overwhelming.

He cataloged pressure points, vulnerable joints, the most efficient way to incapacitate without killing. Then, the most painful ways to kill.

"That's why you flinched," he murmured, forcing his voice to remain neutral despite the violence churning beneath his sternum.

She nodded. "Old habits. Trauma response. Amygdala hijack—my body remembers even when my prefrontal cortex knows better." She straightened, mask sliding back into place. "Anyway, ancient history. I escaped. Rebuilt my life, my career. There's no permanent damage except an aversion to men who think they know better than I do about my life."

"Which is why you objected to this arrangement."

"One of many reasons." She met his gaze directly. "I don't like being controlled. For any reason."

"Understood."

And he did understand. Control was its own kind of safety. He controlled his emotions, his reactions, his environment. Blair controlled through analysis, through verbalization, and through scientific certainty.

"I have no interest in controlling you," he said, choosing his words with uncharacteristic care. "The marriage is tactical. Security-focused. Nothing more."

Something flickered in her eyes—relief, perhaps, or disappointment. He couldn't decipher which, and that unsettled him more than an unidentified target in hostile territory.

"Well, at least we're on the same page," she said, pushing away from the table. "I should get ready for the meeting."

Tanner nodded, gathering the plates as she headed toward the bathroom. The domestic routine felt unfamiliar but not entirely unpleasant. A complication he hadn't anticipated.

His phone vibrated with an alert from the building's security system. Package delivery requiring a signature. He checked the security feed on his phone: a courier holding a small box, nothing immediately suspicious. The delivery uniform appeared regulation, posture indicating civilian rather than operative, no visible weapons bulge.

"Package delivery," he called to Blair. "I'll handle it."

Her acknowledgment came muffled through the bathroom door.

Tanner took the stairs rather than the elevator, standard protocol when approaching unknown deliveries. The courier waited in the lobby, expression bored, weight shifted to one hip; posture suggesting civilian rather than operative. Still, Tanner conducted a subtle assessment as he approached: hands relaxed, not hovering near concealed

weapons; eyes scanning the environment but not with tactical awareness; breathing pattern consistent with boredom rather than pre-
mission tension.

"Delivery for Dr. Blair Winters," the courier said, holding out a
digital signature pad.

"Whitney," Tanner corrected automatically. "Dr. Blair Whitney."

"Oh." The courier checked his device. "System still shows Winters.
Whatever, man. Just need a signature."

Tanner signed, accepting the small package. Standard courier
service packaging, proper labeling, nothing visibly suspicious. Weight
distribution consistent with documents rather than devices. No tick-
ing. No chemical smell. He'd scan it before bringing it upstairs.

Twenty minutes later, the package—cleared through portable scanning equipment—sat on the kitchen counter while Tanner waited for
Blair to emerge from the bathroom.

When she finally appeared, hair damp from the shower and
wearing a simple blouse and slacks, she looked more like herself; the
composed scientist rather than the vulnerable woman from earlier.
The transformation was impressive, like watching a soldier suit up for
combat.

"What's that?" she asked, noticing the package.

"Delivery for you. I cleared it." He gestured toward the sender
information. "It's from your lab colleague. Constantine."

"My research assistant?" Blair approached cautiously. "I didn't give
him this address."

"Routed through the Crest Strategies mail system. Security
protocol."

She carefully opened the package, fingers working with the precise
movements of someone accustomed to handling delicate laboratory
specimens. Inside were a thumb drive and a handwritten note. Her
eyes widened as she read it, pupils dilating with excitement.

"It's data from our latest trial," she said, her voice accelerating
with each word. "Constantine managed to copy it before they seized
everything. This is... this could be crucial for continuing my work."

Tanner watched her expression transform, the scientist emerging fully now. Her eyes brightened, her movements became more animated, and her verbal processing kicked into high gear.

"The protein markers in the final trial showed a 78% increase in neural pathway regeneration across the C4-C7 vertebral sections. If I can correlate this with the previous dosage response curve..." She paused, looking up at Tanner with genuine gratitude. "Thank you for getting this to me."

He nodded, uncomfortable with her thanks. "Just doing my job."

"Well, your job just gave me hope for the first time in days." She clutched the thumb drive as if it contained launch codes rather than research data.

As she turned to set the package aside, something slipped from beneath the packing material—a folded piece of paper that hadn't been part of the note. Tanner reached for it at the same time Blair did, their fingers brushing. This time, neither pulled away immediately.

Blair unfolded the paper, her expression shifting from excitement to confusion to fear in rapid succession, like watching a controlled detonation in slow motion.

"What the fuck?" she whispered, the color draining from her face.

Tanner took the paper from her trembling fingers. A single sentence, printed in plain text:

We know where you are. Marriage won't save you or your research.

Rage boiled up instantly. Not the cold tactical anger he was accustomed to, but something primal and protective that bypassed strategic assessment.

Blair. Threatened. Unacceptable.

Tanner's mind snapped into combat mode. Threat assessment. Security protocols. Extraction options. The burn of adrenaline coursed through his system, sharpening his senses.

"Stay here." He moved to the door, weapon already in hand, preparing to check the hallway, the elevator, any point of access. His heart hammered not with fear but with the terrible clarity of imminent violence.

"How did they find me?" Blair's voice had lost its earlier confidence, shrinking into something small and vulnerable that made his trigger finger itch. "How did they know about the marriage? It just happened yesterday."

Valid questions. Concerning implications.

"Security breach. Internal or external." He checked his weapon, mentally mapping the building's exit routes, calculating kill zones and choke points. "I need to move you to a secondary location."

"Wait." Blair held up the note, her mind already analyzing despite the fear evident in her trembling hands. "This came with Constantine's package, but it's not his handwriting or style. Which means someone intercepted his delivery and added this."

"When did he send it?"

"According to his note, two days ago." She paled further, freckles standing out like target designations against suddenly ashen skin. "Before the wedding."

The timing suggested knowledge of their plans. Which meant a leak within Crest Strategies.

"Pack essential items," Tanner instructed, his voice dropping. "We're leaving in five minutes."

"But the meeting—"

"Compromised." He was already texting Benedict, using encrypted channels.

> Safe location compromised. Note with knowledge of marriage. Internal leak suspected. Moving location. Report only through secure channels.

Blair moved quickly, gathering the few personal items she'd accumulated. Tanner appreciated her efficiency, the way she asked no further questions despite the fear evident in her movements. The ability to function under pressure—rare in civilians, invaluable in combat situations.

Three minutes later, they were ready. Tanner checked the hallway, then motioned for Blair to follow. They took the service elevator to the parking garage, where Tanner led her to a vehicle different from the one they'd arrived in—a nondescript gray sedan with reinforced doors and bulletproof glass.

"It's protocol in situations like yours for your security to switch up vehicles from time to time," he explained, helping her into the passenger seat, hyperaware of the softness of her elbow beneath his palm.

Blair nodded, clutching her bag to her chest. "So you expected this."

"Prepared for it," he corrected, starting the engine. "It's different."

As they pulled out of the garage, Tanner kept his focus on potential surveillance, tail vehicles, anything unusual. The weight of his weapon against his side was reassuring, a reminder that he could protect her.

Would protect her.

Blair remained silent beside him, which was concerning in itself. Her typical verbal processing had gone quiet, suggesting heightened stress levels. The absence of her constant analysis created a vacuum that amplified the tension in the vehicle.

"You're safe," he said, the words feeling foreign on his tongue. Reassurance wasn't his specialty. "This is procedural. Precautionary."

She looked at him, eyes wide, pulse visibly racing at the base of her throat. "Someone knows about us. Knows where I am. Knows about the marriage. And they're threatening me anyway."

"Yes."

"So our whole plan—the marriage, the legal protection—it might not work."

"The plan remains valid," he insisted, with more conviction than he felt. "This is a countermeasure. We adapt."

They drove in silence for several minutes before Blair spoke again.

"Where are we going?"

"Secondary safe house. More isolated. Enhanced security."

"And if that's compromised too?"

"We have over thirty safe houses in the state of New York. If we run out of those, we move out of state."

Despite everything, she gave a short laugh that released some of the tension coiled in the car. "You really do have contingencies for your contingencies."

"It's my job."

"To protect me," she said softly.

"Yes."

"Because I'm your assignment."

"Yes." Tanner's hands tightened on the steering wheel until the leather creaked in protest. "And you're my wife."

Legally accurate but emotionally complex. A designation with unexpected personal resonance.

"Temporarily," she reminded him, though her voice lacked conviction.

Tanner didn't respond. His attention had shifted to the side mirror, where a black sedan had maintained the same distance behind them for the past several turns. Could be coincidence. Could be surveillance.

"Hold on," he instructed, making a sudden left turn without signaling.

The sedan copied.

"We're being followed?" Blair's voice rose slightly, the pitch shifting from scientist to frightened civilian.

"Potentially." He made another abrupt turn, accelerating through an amber light.

The sedan matched their movements, closing the distance. Fuck, it was likely a professional driver. They were maintaining an optimal pursuit position. It didn't help that the windows were tinted beyond legal limits, concealing the number and armament of occupants.

"Damn it," Tanner said, his voice hardening. "Hold on."

He executed a series of rapid maneuvers—sharp turns, acceleration, deceleration—designed to lose a tail or force them to reveal themselves as more than casual followers. The sedan stayed with them.

Blair pressed herself back against the seat, one hand gripping the door handle, the other braced against the dashboard. Her breathing sped up, pupils dilated. But she remained silent, allowing him to focus on evasion tactics.

Tanner reached for his phone, pressing a single button that sent an automated alert to the Crest Strategies security team. Then he dropped into the cold clarity of combat mode, awareness expanding to encompass every variable in their environment.

"What do we do?" Blair asked, her knuckles white where she gripped the door handle.

"You don't do anything. I lose them," Tanner replied, voice steady despite the adrenaline now coursing through his system. "Then we go dark until I verify security parameters."

"What if you can't lose them?" The question wasn't accusatory—just a scientist assessing worst-case scenarios.

Tanner's mouth tightened. "I will."

He navigated through a series of alleys and one-way streets, using the city's infrastructure to his advantage. The sedan fell back, temporarily lost, giving Tanner the opening he needed to access an underground parking structure with multiple exits.

As they descended into the dimly lit garage, Blair's breathing finally slowed. "Are they gone?"

"Temporarily." Tanner stayed silent until they emerged from a different exit, the sedan nowhere in sight. He continued evasive driving for another twenty minutes before pulling into a residential neighborhood.

"We're here," he said, parking behind a modest duplex.

Blair nodded, her breath coming faster than normal. He recognized the early signs of an anxiety response; elevated respiration, dilated pupils, minute tremors in her hands. Symptoms that in a combat situation would indicate a soldier about to break under pressure.

"Blair." He'd rarely used her first name, the intimacy of it still uncomfortable on his tongue. "Focus on my voice. You're safe. I've got you."

Her eyes locked on his, seeking stability in the storm. "I'm fine."

"Bullshit."

That surprised a small laugh out of her. "Such language, Mr. Whitney."

"You've said worse."

"True." She took a deep breath, visibly centering herself.

They exited the vehicle, Tanner maintaining proximity without crowding her. The duplex looked ordinary from the outside, which was exactly the point. Nothing about it suggested a safe house operated by one of the most elite security firms in the country.

Inside, the space was small but functional. Basic furnishings, a stocked kitchen, security features disguised as standard household fixtures. The air smelled of lemon cleaner and the faint metallic scent of recently oiled weapons. Tanner conducted a quick sweep while Blair stood in the entryway.

"All clear," he announced, holstering his weapon. "Security systems active."

Blair nodded, setting her bag down. "Now what?"

"We wait. I contacted Benedict through secure channels. We'll verify the next steps."

She wrapped her arms around herself, suddenly looking smaller in the unfamiliar space. "I should have known it wouldn't be that simple. Nothing in my life ever is."

Tanner moved toward her without conscious decision, drawn by the vulnerability in her posture. He stopped just short of touching her, muscle memory from a lifetime of maintaining distance warring with an unfamiliar impulse to provide comfort.

"We planned for this."

"You planned for this," she corrected, meeting his gaze with unexpected directness. "I was busy adjusting to the idea of being married to a stranger."

Something about her vulnerability in that moment broke through his tactical focus. Without analyzing the impulse, he reached out, his hand settling on her shoulder. The contact was meant to be reassuring, professional. It wasn't supposed to send awareness cascading through his system like a firefight's hypervigilance.

Blair looked up at him, surprise evident in her eyes. "You're touching me."

"Tactical reassurance."

"Is that what they taught you in special ops? How to tactically reassure a frightened civilian?" Her tone shifted from vulnerability to the scientific skepticism that seemed to be her own defensive mechanism.

The corner of his mouth twitched. "No."

Her gaze dropped to his hand on her shoulder, then back to his face. "So this is... improvisation?"

"Something like that."

He should remove his hand. The contact had exceeded operational necessity. But the warmth beneath his palm kept him anchored, the slight tremor in her body triggering protective instincts that went beyond obligation. The need to shield her from threats felt less like mission parameters and more like something elemental, something he hadn't felt since before Kandahar.

"Thank you," she said quietly. "For getting us out of there. For being prepared."

Tanner nodded, finally withdrawing his hand. The loss of contact left an unexpected void, like a phantom limb sensation after amputation.

"I should contact Benedict, again," he said, moving toward the secured communications equipment concealed behind a false panel in the living room wall.

Blair watched him go, her expression unreadable. "Right. Of course."

As he established the secure connection, Tanner's focus was compromised. The mission parameters remained clear: protect Blair Winters—Whitney—and her research at all costs. But something had shifted, a complication he hadn't accounted for in his assessment.

Benedict's face appeared on the secure tablet. "Status?"

"We're secure at location Location Charlie. I lost the tail vehicle. The doctor is safe."

Benedict nodded. "Good. Penn is investigating the leak. Our initial assessment suggests the interception of the package rather than internal breach. Still, you two should stay put until we have confirmation."

"Understood. Timeline?"

"Not sure yet. Cars still wants public appearances from you two eventually, but I'm trying to get him to push it out until we can figure out what the hell that was. I'll contact you through this channel only. Stay safe, man."

The connection ended.

Fuck. And undetermined amount of time stuck in close quarters with Blair. In a safe house with limited space. One bedroom. One bed. A tactical situation that shouldn't trigger the rush of awareness currently traveling his nervous system.

He turned to find her standing in the kitchen, examining the sparse contents of the refrigerator. The sunlight through dusty blinds caught in her hair, highlighting strands of copper among the dark curls. An irrelevant detail that his brain cataloged anyway.

"Benedict just told me we're supposed to stay here until they figure some things out," he informed her. "Penn's investigating the source of the leak."

Blair nodded, closing the refrigerator door. "So we're stuck here."

"Yes."

"There's only one bedroom," she said, glancing toward the only other door besides the bathroom. "I'm guessing one bed."

"I'll take the couch."

She studied him, head tilting in a way that reminded him of intelligence analysts assessing satellite imagery. "Are you always the martyr?"

"When the situation demands it if me. Besides, as you pointed out, I get up earlier, and the couch is better positioned for me to respond to external threats. And I sleep lightly."

"You really do wake up at an ungodly hour." She moved to the living area, sinking onto the couch in question. The cushions exhaled dust motes that danced in the surrounding sunlight. "What do we do now?"

Tanner checked his watch. "I'll review security protocols. Establish communication guidelines. Assess threat vectors."

"Sounds thrilling," Blair muttered. "No wonder you're so much fun at parties."

Despite everything, Tanner felt that strange twitch at the corner of his mouth again. Her sarcasm was oddly refreshing after years of people too intimidated to speak to him candidly. Most people watched their words around him, as if one wrong phrase might provoke violence. Blair seemed to have no such filter.

"Or," she continued, her fingers tracing nervous patterns on the worn fabric of the couch, "we could use this time to establish some actual human connection, given that we're legally married and potentially in mortal danger and have to give a performance to the world once we're off of house arrest."

"Connection," he repeated, raising an eyebrow. "I don't understand."

"Yes, Tanner. Connection. That thing normal people do when they're not busy being scary robots." She patted the couch beside her. "Sit. Talk to me. Tell me something about yourself that isn't related to security protocols or military operations."

He remained standing, assessing the request. "Why?"

"Because we're stuck here for god knows how long, and I'll lose my mind if I spend it watching you patrol the perimeter and check your weapon every five minutes." She sighed, shoulders slumping. "Plus, I'm scared. My amygdala is in overdrive, cortisol flooding my system. Talking helps me process. You've probably noticed."

That admission—its simple vulnerability—broke through his resistance. Tanner moved to the couch, maintaining a calculated distance as he sat, close enough for conversation but not so close their bodies would touch.

"What do you want to know?"

"Something real," she said. "Something that makes you more than just my security detail with a wedding ring."

Tanner considered. Personal disclosure wasn't his strong suit, but operational parameters had shifted. They were married. There had been a direct threat. Some level of trust was necessary.

"I had a sister," he said finally. "Annabelle."

Blair's expression softened, the scientist momentarily replaced by something warmer. "Older or younger?"

"Younger. Twenty-nine."

"Where is she now? Wait, had?"

Tanner's jaw tightened until he felt tendons creak. "Yes, had."

Understanding dawned in Blair's eyes, her breath catching audibly. "I'm sorry," she said softly. "Were you close?"

"Yes." The word came out rougher than intended, scraped over emotional gravel he'd thought long buried.

"What was she like?"

"Brilliant. She studied neuroscience, like you. Was even recruited by defense contractors after her doctorate. She specialized in research projects." He stared at the wall, seeing memories instead of peeling paint. "It was classified work. Off-book operations she couldn't tell me about."

Blair moved closer, her presence both comforting and unsettling. "What happened to her?"

"They happened to her." His voice hardened, the old rage rising. "They took her to a government black site. She went in brilliant, came out broken."

"And then?"

"PTSD. Couldn't sleep. Couldn't work. Couldn't reconnect." His hands clenched into fists, knuckles whitening. "She took her life three years ago. I went out to visit her and found her in the bathtub. The water was still warm. I was too late."

Blair's sharp intake of breath punctuated the silence that followed. Then, to his surprise, her hand covered his, warm and steady where his was cold and rigid.

"That's why you agreed to this," she said quietly. "To the marriage. You're trying to prevent the same thing from happening to me."

Tanner didn't confirm or deny, but he didn't pull his hand away either. Her touch anchored him in a way he couldn't explain, like a tether preventing freefall.

"I'm sorry about Annabelle," Blair continued. "And I'm grateful you're trying to protect me. Even if the methods are... unorthodox."

The warmth of her hand seeped into his skin, creating an awareness that had nothing to do with assessment and everything to do with the woman beside him. His wife, legally if not emotionally.

"I won't let them take you," he said, the words emerging with a ferocity that surprised even him. "Not like they took her."

"I believe you," Blair replied, and the simple conviction in her voice penetrated barriers he'd maintained for years. "Thank you for sharing that with me."

Her fingers tightened around his. Tanner turned his hand, almost unconsciously, until their palms pressed together, fingers intertwining.

The contact should have been uncomfortable. Unnecessary physical proximity, potential emotional compromise. Instead, it felt like the most natural position he'd ever assumed.

Blair's pulse quickened beneath his fingertips—elevated but not distressed. Her pupils dilated slightly, respiration increasing. Physiological responses suggesting something beyond fear or anxiety.

"You're touching me again," she whispered.

"Yes."

"Are you blurring professional boundaries?"

"Potentially."

She smiled faintly. "Back to single words. At least some things remain consistent."

Tanner studied the curve of her lips, the way her pulse visibly fluttered at the base of her throat, the slight flush spreading across her cheeks. Shit. She was beautiful. His gaze dropped to her lips and—oh, fuck. Why the hell did she have to suck the corner of her bottom lip between her teeth? It was too fucking sexy. God, did she know she was doing that? He forced his gaze to meet her eyes again, and damn it, she was staring at his mouth too.

"Operational parameters often shift based on conditions," he said, not entirely sure what he was trying to justify.

"Is that your way of saying the rules change?" She asked, meeting his gaze again briefly before dropping back to his lips.

"Are you okay with that?"

"I suppose some rules could hypothetically be altered."

A moment of silence stretched between them. The safe house creaked around them, the wood settling, but Tanner registered only the sound of Blair's breathing, slightly accelerated, and the steady pressure of her hand in his.

Blair's free hand reached up, hesitating just short of touching his face. "May I?" she asked.

Tanner nodded once.

Her fingertips traced the scar bisecting his eyebrow, the touch feather-light but sending awareness cascading through his system.

"How did you get this?" she asked.

"IED. Kandahar. Shrapnel." His breath caught as her fingers continued their exploration. "Seven men in my unit. Three didn't make it."

She nodded, accepting the clipped explanation where others would have pressed for details. Her touch continued, tracing the line of his jaw, the tension in his neck, coming to rest at his pulse point where his heartbeat betrayed his outward calm.

"Your heart's racing," she observed. "Am I bothering you?"

"No."

"Oh," she said, moving back. "Good," Blair said, her voice steady despite the flush deepening on her cheeks. "Still, I don't know what I was thinking. Of course your heart is racing. You're probably thinking of a million different safety protocols or where to go next or something else and I'm distracting you by digging into your past and asking invasive questions. Shit, Tanner, I'm sorry." She tried to pull away more, but he caught her wrist.

"Don't."

"Don't what?" She asked, her focus on his hand gently holding hers.

"Don't apologize. You've done nothing wrong."

Their faces were closer now, the distance between them diminishing without conscious decision. Tanner cataloged every detail. The gold flecks in her hazel eyes, the faint freckle near her temple, the curve of her upper lip. Fuck, those lips were perfect. Hypnotizing, even as she rambled on and on and on.

"I have a dumb question."

"Are there dumb questions?" Tanner asked, still watching her cherry pink mouth.

"Have you ever worked with children? Yes. There are absolutely dumb questions. And this is one of them."

When he glanced back up at her eyes, she was watching him with a wince already ingrained into her features. "Ask it."

"You're not going to hate me afterwards?"

"Not a fortune teller. I'm a security specialist. Ask the damn question." His focus dropped back to her lips again in anticipation.

"Fine. Just... don't hate me." She paused, and he waited, enamoured by the way she chewed on her bottom lip. Finally, she spoke. "Would it be smart to practice a kiss in case we have to do it publicly? You know, to serve as evidence of our perfect, not at all suspicious marriage?"

For a moment, he thought he might smile. Might chuckle. Damn, she was good at making him want to do that. Instead, Tanner's hand moved to cup her face. "I believe that's a completely a reasonable idea."

"Great," she breathed against his thumb as he traced that infuriating bottom lip. "Then should we..."

He hesitated just for a moment before closing the distance between them. His lips met Blair's in a slow, testing brush, his breathing measured despite the sound of his pulse crashing in his ears. He registered the warmth of her mouth, the faint tremor in his fingers where they cradled her jaw, the electric response of his nervous system when she sighed against him. This was reconnaissance. Evidence gathering. Necessary for the success of their marriage cover story.

They parted barely, her breath ghosting over his lips, her eyes searching his.

"Did that"—her voice hitched—"seem convincing enough for public scenarios?"

"There's a chance it needs refinement." The words came out as more of a grunt than anything. His thumb brushed the hinge of her jaw, tracing the rapid flutter beneath her skin. Every muscle in his body tightened when her fingers curled into the front of his shirt.

"It would need to be convincing," she whispered against him.

"It would. So do you want to try again, or—"

Without warning, Blair surged forward, pressing her mouth to his. Their first kiss had been experimentation. This was an ambush. His fingers tangled in her hair, angling her head back as her teeth caught his lower lip. All rational thought evaporated—protocols, objectives, his carefully maintained detachment—incinerated by the way she arched against him.

Her fingertips mapped the scars along his nape. Distantly, he registered the press of her thigh against his growing hardness. Shit. Shit. Shit. God, he had a fucking erection for this woman. Damn it. She was his mission. Part of his job. The kiss was a mistake, and the hardness in his pants was a miscalculation he'd failed to account for.

Tanner tore himself away, pulse pounding

"A perimeter check. I'm going to—" His voice was gravel, and he cleared it. "Just stay here."

He was out the door before she could respond. Before the dangerous swell of emotion in his chest could breach containment. The retreat was necessary.

Justifiable.

Even if all he could still taste was her.

CHAPTER FIVE

BLAIR

TWO WEEKS. IT'D BEEN TWO WEEKS SINCE SHE HAD KISSED Tanner. Two weeks since he'd spoken more than just a handful of words to her. He'd kept his word and slept on the couch every night. By the time she woke up in the morning, he'd long since been up, checking the exits and perimeter every fifteen minutes. Like an uneasy guard dog.

Every time Tanner entered a room, Blair's anterior cingulate cortex lit up like a Christmas tree. Hardly two weeks of marriage, and she'd become a walking neurochemical disaster.

Blair tracked the sound of Tanner's footsteps as he completed his morning security patrol. She'd mapped his patterns like experimental data points; he varied his route by exactly seven minutes each day to avoid establishing a targetable routine.

It was 5 fucking thirty in the morning.

She pressed her face into the pillow, trying to muffle the completely irrational oxytocin response that accompanied his proximity. This marriage was supposed to be a security arrangement, not a dopamine delivery system. Her limbic system clearly hadn't gotten the memo.

Flopping onto her back, the ceiling of the bedroom came into focus as Blair forced herself to full consciousness. Location Charlie, as Tanner insisted on calling it, was significantly more livable than their previous safe house. Despite only having one bedroom, Tanner had surprised her the second day by showing her the small shed outside. Only, it wasn't a shed. It was a rudimentary lab.

Of course, it wasn't fully outfitted, and she'd need more equipment, but it was enough to start her work again. Not that remote work compared to an actual laboratory environment. Without proper equipment, she could only analyze Constantine's data, not generate new findings. Like a chef restricted to reading recipes without cooking. No, the small lab was nice, but only to distract her. To keep busy. To keep her mind from wandering to dangerous thoughts like the potential threats on her life and the way Tanner had kissed her. The way his lips had brought something she'd thought was dead within her back to life.

A scientific impossibility. It must've been a mistake in the wiring of her brain. Her ex-husband had made damn sure she'd never trust a man enough again to give that vulnerable part of herself.

She just needed her vibrator. Needed to relieve some stress. Too bad she didn't have it, and her current husband was constantly near enough to hear if she were doing self-maintenance.

For a moment, she wondered what sort of response Tanner might have if he did overhear her. A strange experiment she unfortunately couldn't—no, *wouldn't*—complete.

The floorboards in the hallway creaked. It appeared Tanner had finished clearing the eastern perimeter of their safe house. He moved differently outdoors versus indoors, a detail her brain refused to stop cataloging despite its complete irrelevance to anything that mattered.

Blair swung her legs over the side of the bed, wincing as her bare feet met the cold hardwood. She sighed. After two weeks, she had hoped her body would, respectfully, calm the fuck down. She was tired of analyzing her own biochemical responses like a particularly frustrating experiment with contaminated variables.

The most maddening part was how predictable her reactions had become. Elevated heart rate: 12.7 beats per minute above baseline whenever he entered a room. Pupillary dilation: approximately 20% increase when making direct eye contact. Core temperature increase: 0.4 degrees when accidental physical contact occurred.

Her body had become a traitor to her rational mind.

Blair waited for another fifteen minutes before she heard Tanner leave to check the perimeter again before she padded to the bathroom and turned the shower to its hottest setting. Perhaps that would help calm her racing thoughts.

It didn't.

She'd just finished brushing her teeth when three precise knocks sounded at the bathroom door.

"Yes?" She tightened the belt of her robe.

"Carson called. He wants us to meet at headquarters. Ten hundred hours." Tanner's voice carried through the door, that deep baritone that somehow resonated at a frequency that triggered her insular cortex. "Reputation rehabilitation strategy."

Blair rolled her eyes. Of course. Carson had been messaging daily about "managing the narrative" and "strategic positioning," as if her life's work could be reduced to PR talking points and media spin.

"You mean we get to leave suburban hell?" She asked, and could've sworn she heard a snort.

"Yes."

"I'll be ready," she called back.

"Breakfast in fifteen."

His footsteps retreated. Two weeks ago, she might have tried to analyze those footsteps, searching for micro-variations that might indicate his emotional state. Now she knew better. Her husband maintained control at a level that would impress a neurosurgeon during a delicate procedure.

Except for that one moment, when control had fractured just enough to glimpse the man beneath the tactical exterior.

Well, the man and his member.

God, he'd been huge and hard against her thigh as he'd tightened his hands in her hair and around her waist. As they'd breathed the same air. As he'd kissed her without an ounce of hesitation.

Blair shook her head, water droplets spattering the bathroom tiles. "What the hell?" She whispered, chastising herself under her breath as she got dressed. "Today is about dissecting the inappropriate serotonin surges I get when I'm around my temporary husband. Today is about salvaging my damn reputation and research. Those are the only things that actually matter. Come on, Blair. Keep it together."

Twenty-two minutes later, showered and dressed in clothes that someone else had arranged—all perfectly in her size and preferred style, which raised disturbing questions about Crest Strategies' surveillance capabilities—Blair made her way to the kitchen. The scent of coffee and something distinctly non-MRE-like filled the air.

Tanner stood at the stove, his back to her, the muscles beneath his fitted black t-shirt shifting as he flipped something in a cast iron pan. The Glock holstered at his hip created a jarring contrast with the domestic scene, like a Renaissance painting where a tattooed warrior prepared breakfast.

"Something smells like actual food," she said, announcing her presence though she knew he'd registered her approach from the moment the door opened.

"Protein. Carbohydrates. Essential nutrients." His standard response, though she caught the faint twitch at the corner of his mouth that she'd learned to identify as his version of a smile.

"You're cooking actual food instead of nutrition packets. I'm impressed." Blair moved to the coffeemaker, calculating her trajectory to maintain precisely 2.5 feet of separation; close enough for normal interaction, far enough to minimize those inconvenient pheromonal responses. "Progress in your civilian reintegration."

Tanner slid a plate toward her—eggs with peppers and spinach, whole grain toast, sliced fruit arranged in a way that managed to be both amusing and oddly endearing. "It's healthy."

"Of course." She took the plate, miscalculating the distance. Their fingers brushed, sending a cascade of electrical activity through her somatosensory cortex that her cerebellum immediately cataloged as irrelevant data. "So we're being briefed today on Carson's PR strategy?"

"Yes." Tanner sat across from her, his own plate notably more protein-heavy. "Your preliminary reputation rehabilitation."

"Sounds thrilling." Blair bit into a piece of toast to hide her grimace.

"From what Benedict has told me, Carson believes a controlled interview is the optimal strategy."

Blair groaned, jabbing her fork into an innocent piece of egg. "Let me guess. Carefully scripted answers, rehearsed facial expressions, strategic tears? Perhaps I should practice looking contrite but determined in the mirror."

"Likely."

"Great. Because nothing says 'trust me with experimental neural compounds' like a performance worthy of community theater."

This time, Tanner's mouth definitely twitched. The microexpression was gone in milliseconds, but Blair caught it.

They ate in relative silence, the only sounds being cutlery against plates and Blair's occasional muttering about reputation management versus scientific integrity. The quiet should have been uncomfortable, but somehow it wasn't. In two weeks, they'd developed a strange equilibrium; her constant verbal processing balanced by his silence. It worked, in an odd way.

"I need to get ready. We leave in ten minutes," Tanner said, collecting their empty plates. He disappeared into the bedroom, moving to the bathroom a moment later.

When he emerged, Tanner wore a charcoal suit that emphasized the breadth of his shoulders, his usual tactical gear concealed beneath expertly tailored fabric. For the first time since their wedding, she remembered that he wasn't just some security specialist. Tanner was also one of the five men in charge of Crest Strategies. Maybe he wasn't Carson Crest, but he was still a very powerful man. And a billionaire. It was impressive how easily he hid that though, unlike Carson, Benedict, and James. Penn seemed to hide it well too, even though he also was just as powerful as his brethren.

"Is something wrong?" he asked, gesturing to the outfit.

"Not at all." Blair forced her attention back to his face from where it had been studying certain areas of him. The trousers were... fitted, which was a detail she'd noted when he'd leaned over the table to grab his keys. Damn. His ass was a perfect specimen.

"Let's get this over with," he said, opening the front door for her.

The drive to Crest Strategies took forty-seven minutes, during which Blair rehearsed potential questions and answers aloud while Tanner listened in what she'd come to recognize as attentive silence. His occasional nods or minute frowns provided more feedback than most people's lengthy critiques.

Suburbia gradually gave way to urban density as they approached Manhattan. Through the bulletproof windows, the city looked deceptively normal. People rushed to work. Delivery trucks sat double-parked. Apparently, the rhythm of commerce had continued while her entire life remained in suspended animation.

As they pulled into the underground parking garage, Blair's verbal cascade finally slowed. "I hate this," she admitted, her fingers twisting a loose thread on her blazer sleeve. "Being coached on how to sound genuine when discussing my life's work. The whole concept is contradictory. Authenticity cannot, by definition, be performative."

Tanner parked, turning to face her fully for the first time that morning. The garage's fluorescent lighting cast harsh shadows across his face, emphasizing the scar that bisected his eyebrow.

"Be who you are," he mumbled. "Not who they expect."

The simplicity of the statement, coming from a man who communicated primarily in fragments, left her momentarily speechless. Before she could respond, he was out of the car, circling to open her door.

"Let's go, Doctor."

———

"ABSOLUTELY NOT," CARSON SAID, HIS TONE LEAVING NO room for argument. "We need controlled, measured responses. The public is fickle, Dr. Winters. One emotional outburst, one unscripted moment, and we lose the narrative." Carson finished speaking.

Blair sat at the conference table, surrounded by the full Crest Strategies team. Benedict had presented a comprehensive analysis of her reputation damage—charts showing social media sentiment (83% negative, 12% neutral, 5% positive), scientific community response (67% skeptical, 22% withholding judgment, 11% supportive), and media coverage (overwhelmingly hostile). The visual representation of her professional destruction, rendered in cold percentages and down-ward-trending graphs, made her stomach clench.

"Whitney," Tanner corrected from his position by the door.

Everyone turned to look at him.

"Her name," Tanner said simply. "Dr. Whitney. Not Winters."

A strange warmth spread through Blair's chest at the correction, a vasodilation response that had nothing to do with room temperature. She'd nearly forgotten that technically, legally, her name had changed with their marriage.

"Right," Carson continued, raising an eyebrow at Tanner before he resettled his focus on Blair. "Dr. Whitney. The point remains. This interview is carefully orchestrated. Megan DeLancy from SciTech Review is sympathetic to our position. She'll ask the questions we've approved, and you'll give the answers we've prepared." He slid a folder toward Blair. "Your script."

Blair opened it, scanning the sanitized, corporate responses that bore no resemblance to her actual thoughts or feelings. Words like "miscommunication" and "regrettable misunderstanding" jumped out at her like red flags in experimental data.

"I appreciate the forethought, Mr. Crest, but these aren't my words," she said, tracing one particularly egregious sentence with her finger. "This isn't even my speech pattern."

"They're better than your words," Carson replied. "They're words that test well with focus groups. They're words that redirect away from controversy and toward reconciliation."

"Focus groups." Blair's voice flattened. "You tested how I should explain my life's work with random people who likely can't distin-guish between a neuron and a nephron?"

"Not random. Carefully selected demographics representing key stakeholder groups in your reputation rehabilitation." Carson's smile was professional but cold, the facial equivalent of a placebo. "Trust the process, Dr. Whitney. We do this for a living."

Before she could argue again, James began outlining the legal strategy.

"We've filed preliminary motions challenging the seizure of your research materials on procedural grounds. However, the most effective approach is shifting public opinion."

"Hence the interview," Benedict added. "Megan DeLancy's audience includes key scientific community influencers. If they start questioning the bioweapon narrative, others will follow. It's basic social influence theory applied to specialized communities."

Blair gave a small nod. Logically, the strategy made sense, even if the scripted responses turned her stomach like an adverse reaction to experimental compounds. "When is this interview?"

Carson checked his watch. "One hour. Hair and makeup team is waiting down the hall."

"Hair and—" Blair started to protest, but Carson had already moved on.

"Benedict will prep you on delivery. Remember, the goal is to appear contrite but confident, apologetic but authoritative. Sincere about patient welfare but not defensive about regulatory oversight."

"So basically, be a walking contradiction," Blair muttered.

"Be whatever the situation requires," Carson corrected. "That's how you get your research back. That's how you resume helping patients."

The meeting continued with specific instructions—how to sit (straight but not rigid, suggesting openness), how to maintain eye contact (direct but not challenging), how to modulate her voice (warm but authoritative). Blair felt increasingly like an experimental subject being conditioned for optimal response.

When they broke for final preparations, Blair escaped to the bathroom, splashing cold water on her neck. The shock of it cleared her head momentarily, water droplets tracking down her skin. A stylist had arranged her naturally chaotic curls into something more controlled, applied makeup that enhanced without being obvious. She looked polished, professional, and oddly disconnected from herself.

The bathroom door opened, and she expected to see the makeup artist coming to touch up her face. Instead, Tanner appeared, closing the door behind him.

"This is the women's restroom," she pointed out.

"Secured the perimeter." His version of an explanation. "You're stressed."

It wasn't a question. He'd become unsettlingly adept at reading her physiological responses. The fact that he could interpret her cortisol levels from microexpressions was both impressive and deeply inconvenient.

"I feel like a fraud," Blair admitted, gripping the edge of the counter. "They want me to apologize for things I didn't do, to speak in carefully calibrated sound bites crafted to manipulate emotional responses. That's not how science works. That's not who I am."

Tanner moved closer, his reflection appearing behind hers in the mirror. The contrast between them was almost comical. Her nervous energy versus his controlled stillness, her expressive features versus his composed mask.

"Earlier advice still applies."

"Be who I am, not who they expect," she quoted. "Easy for you to say. You're not the one whose career is hanging by a thread. You're not the one who has to convince the world you weren't creating bioweapons in your spare time."

"Authenticity resonates." Tanner's eyes met hers in the mirror. "Humans evolved to recognize deception. You're already an authentic person. Just be you, otherwise people will clock it right away."

Blair turned only to come face to face with his chest. She tilted her head up to look at him, close enough to detect the minty scent of his breath, the faint aroma of gun oil that always seemed to cling to him. "Carson will be pissed."

"Carson isn't god, thank fuck. He may play at it, but he isn't." Tanner's gaze held hers. "Your research matters because it's real. You matter because you're real."

Blair's mouth opened, but no words came out. This man, who calculated every word like ammunition to be conserved, had just offered the most genuine encouragement she'd received since her world collapsed.

"Thank you," she whispered. For one moment, her gaze dropped to his mouth. She caught herself though, and refocused on his eyes.

Tanner nodded once, then stepped back, resuming his professional distance. "The interview is in ten minutes. I'll be positioned in the room."

He left, and Blair stared at the door for a long moment. Who the hell was this man she'd married?

———

BLAIR SAT IN THE DESIGNATED CHAIR FOR THE INTERVIEW, trying not to fidget as people adjusted the microphones and checked the camera angles. The lights generated more heat than she'd expected, making her hyperaware of the sweat dripping down her spine.

Megan DeLancy, the SciTech Review journalist, was a poised woman in her forties with sharp eyes and a neutral expression that revealed nothing. After brief introductions, they settled into position for the interview.

Carson stood just off-camera, his expression making it clear he expected adherence to the script. Benedict monitored from behind a laptop, presumably tracking real-time response metrics. Tanner positioned himself against the wall, his presence unobtrusive but unmistakable. Penn and James were absent.

"We're live in three, two..." The producer signaled, and the interview began.

The hot lights created a bubble, isolating Blair and Megan in a pool of artificial brightness while the rest of the room faded to shadow. Blair could feel the weight of multiple gazes; the camera's unblinking eye, Carson's expectant stare, Tanner's steady observation.

"Dr. Whitney, thank you for speaking with me today," Megan began, her tone professionally warm.

"Thank you for having me, Ms. DeLancy."

"Please call me Megan. So let's get down to business, shall we? The scientific community was shocked by allegations that your neural regeneration research might have applications as a bioweapon. How do you respond to these claims?"

Blair glanced down at the script, where the carefully crafted response waited: *"There has been an unfortunate misunderstanding regarding the applications of my research. While I regret any confusion, I want to assure everyone that VX-7 was developed exclusively for therapeutic purposes..."*

The sanitized words swam before her eyes. She could recite them perfectly, hitting every focus-group-tested emotional note. She could see Carson nodding encouragingly, practically mouthing the words along with her.

Her gaze shifted to Tanner, the shadow who watched her from the side of the room. *Be who you are, not who they expect.*

Blair set the script aside.

"The allegations are false," she said, her spine straightening as she committed to honesty. "My research has never had offensive applications, and the molecular structure of VX-7, while sharing some superficial similarities to nerve agents, functions completely differently on a cellular level."

Carson's eyes widened, but the momentum of truth carried her forward.

"The whistleblower report deliberately omitted the protein markers that prevent systemic toxicity. As I've said before, it's like comparing water to hydrogen peroxide. They also have similar molecular components, but completely differ in functions and effects. One hydrates cells; the other destroys them."

Megan leaned forward, her professional neutrality shifting to genuine interest. "Yet the review panel found enough evidence to seize your research and shut down your lab."

Blair took a deep breath, the warm studio air filling her lungs. "The panel made their decision based on incomplete information provided by someone with an agenda. I believe my research was targeted because of its commercial potential, not because of any legitimate safety concerns."

"That's a serious accusation," Megan noted.

"It's a serious situation," Blair countered. "My lab was developing a compound that has shown 78% neural regeneration in subjects with complete C4 spinal severance. Do you know what that means?"

Megan shook her head.

"It means people who were told they would never walk again might have a chance at recovery. It means patients with devastating nerve damage might regain function." Blair's hands moved as she spoke, fingers tracing neural pathways in the air. "The VX-7 compound targets damaged myelin sheaths specifically through protein markers that prevent it from affecting healthy tissue. Someone is trying to control that research by discrediting me, and the people who will suffer most are the patients who could benefit from this treatment. That's why it's so important that I be able to resume my research as soon as possible."

From the corner of her eye, Blair could see Carson making a cutting motion, silently urging her to return to the script. She ignored him, the weight of truth carrying her forward like a current.

"Tell me about the therapeutic applications," Megan said, clearly intrigued.

For the next several minutes, Blair explained her research in accessible terms—the targeted nature of VX-7, the successful trial results, the potential revolutionary impact on spinal injury treatment. As she spoke, her hands animated her points.

The heat from the studio lights faded from her awareness as she lost herself in explaining the science she loved. This was her element —translating complex neurobiological concepts into language others could understand. Not reciting focus-group platitudes.

"It sounds remarkable," Megan said, and the genuine interest in her voice was unmistakable. "Which makes these allegations all the more concerning. How has this affected you personally?"

This was dangerous territory. The script contained a carefully measured response about professional disappointment and determination to clear her name.

Instead, Blair said, "It's been devastating. Five years of work, suddenly characterized as something sinister. I've had colleagues distance themselves. Friends ghosting me. Even the funding of my lab has been frozen. Those who worked under me were also hurt in the fallout." She swallowed hard. "But the worst part is knowing that while this plays out, patients who could be benefiting from clinical trials are still waiting for hope. People with spinal injuries who might walk again, victims of nerve damage who might regain function—they're the real casualties in this."

Megan nodded, then surprised Blair with an unexpected question. "There have been rumors of your sudden marriage to Tanner Whitney in recent weeks. Some speculate you've attempted to shift the focus from your work with Vx-7 to the marriage as a distraction. Is that true, or is this the way you've found personal support during this crisis?"

Blair tensed, her nervous system immediately on high alert. She glanced at Tanner, standing motionless against the wall, his expression unreadable except for the slight tightening around his eyes.

"I've been fortunate to have enormous support," she said carefully. "In fact, not long after the accusations about my work came out, I... I did in fact get married. Hence the name change," Blair said with a small chuckle. "My husband... He's been the most supportive. A rock for me to cling to in this storm, I suppose. But I'd prefer to keep my personal life private while I focus on clearing my name and resuming my work. That's why we married in secret. I'd hoped it wouldn't interfere too much with the work my lab has been trying to do over the last five years." Blair smiled, though she ground her molars together. It wasn't a complete lie, but it also wasn't the whole truth.

"Of course," Megan returned the smile. "Just one final question. What would you say to the scientific community that's now questioning your research?"

Blair took a deep breath. "I'd say, examine the evidence for yourselves. The molecular structure, test results, and trial data speak for

themselves. Science is about objective evaluation, not rumor or specu-
lation. I welcome scrutiny of my work—real scrutiny, based on
complete information. Because the truth is in the data, and the data
shows that VX-7 could change lives for the better."

"Thank you, Dr. Whitney. I appreciate your candor."

The interview concluded, and as soon as the cameras stopped
rolling, Carson was at her side.

"What the hell was that?" he demanded in a harsh whisper. "You
completely abandoned the script. You went off-message on every
single question."

"I answered honestly," Blair replied, standing her ground despite
the adrenaline now flooding her system. The post-interview crash left
her feeling shaky but resolute.

"Honesty wasn't the strategy!" Carson's professional veneer
cracked. "We had a carefully calibrated approach—"

"Careful how you speak to her," Tanner said, suddenly next to
Blair. No, not next to her, in front of her. He'd placed himself between
her and Carson. "She did well, right, Ms. DeLancy?"

Megan stared up at Tanner with wide eyes, her gaze dropping to
his left hand. To the ring that matched Blair's.

"Yes," she said, nodding. "She did very well. I'm interested to look
into more of your research, Dr. Whitney." Megan leaned around to get
a better look at Blair behind Tanner. "Thank you for your time, Dr.
Whitney. I hope we can speak again soon."

"Of course. Thank you, Megan," Blair said, pushing past her
husband, who shot her an annoyed look. Ignoring it, Blair shook
Megan's hand and said goodbye. Silence filled the room as Megan and
the rest of the production crew left.

"Cars, Tanner's right. It worked," Benedict said, looking up from
his laptop. "Social media sentiment is shifting. Scientific forums are
picking up her explanation of the molecular structure. Look at this—
#VX7ForPatients is already trending, along with #LetBlairWork."

Carson turned towards Benedict. "What?"

Benedict turned his screen toward them. "These are real-time
analytics. Her explanation of the research is resonating, especially

with the medical community. The focus on patients rather than self-defense is playing extremely well with the general public. The engagement metrics show 47% higher retention than our projections for the scripted responses."

"Let me see that." Carson moved closer, studying the data. "Interesting. We're seeing the first positive sentiment spike since the scandal broke. Technical explanations are being shared widely in scientific communities, with favorable commentary." Carson's expression shifted from anger to calculation in the space of a heartbeat. "Good. Very good."

Blair felt slightly dizzy with the sudden shift. From failure to potential success in the span of minutes.

"The truth worked," she said simply.

Carson studied her with new assessment in his eyes. "Perhaps. But we need to shape this momentum carefully." He turned to Benedict. "Set up a technical briefing for interested science journalists. Controlled environment, but let Dr. Winters speak directly about the research."

"Whitney," Blair corrected, feeling a small surge of satisfaction at the tiny victory.

Carson's lips twitched. "Right. Well, it seems your instincts were better than our focus groups in this instance."

As they discussed next steps, Blair felt a presence at her side. Tanner had moved to stand beside her, close enough that his arm brushed hers. The contact sent a ripple of awareness across her skin, nerve endings firing in unison.

"Good," he breathed, the single word carrying more approval than Carson's strategic pivot.

Blair smiled up at him. "I took your advice."

"Noted."

The return journey to Location Charlie was filled with calls from the Crest team as the positive response continued to build. The car's Bluetooth system relayed Benedict's updates—a former colleague from Cornell had publicly questioned the bioweapon allegations. Three scientific journals were requesting statements. A patient advocacy group for spinal injuries had reached out about partnership opportunities.

As they drove, Blair watched the buildings shrink until they were back in the suburbs. By the time they arrived back at the house, Blair was exhausted but exhilarated. Her reputation wasn't restored, not by a long shot, but for the first time since the scandal broke, she could see a path forward that didn't require sacrificing her integrity.

"You should rest," Tanner said as they entered. "It's been a long day."

"I'm too wired to sleep," Blair admitted, kicking off her heels with a groan of relief. "I'm still processing everything. I don't think I could downregulate my synaptic activity if I tried."

Tanner nodded. "Tea?"

"God, yes. Please."

She followed him to the kitchen. Tanner filled the kettle while she selected the mugs.

"Thank you," she said as he filled her mug. The ceramic was warm against her palms. "Not just for the tea. For the advice. For backing me when I went off-script."

Tanner leaned against the counter, his own mug cradled in hands. Large hands, she noted. Hands that could probably snap a man's neck without effort. Or cause one hell of an orgasm. What the fuck? Where had that thought come from? She cleared her throat, forcing her gaze back to his stoic face.

"You needed to be yourself," he said simply. "Authenticity is your strength."

"Not everyone would agree with that assessment."

"I'm not everyone."

No, he certainly wasn't. Blair studied him over the rim of her mug, the steam creating a momentary veil between them. He was watching her with an intensity that made her stomach twist and heat begin to build even lower.

"Carson wasn't happy I mentioned you," she said, testing the waters. "Or rather, didn't deny your existence."

"Carson has a way of doing things. Whether it's right or not isn't up for me to decide."

"But I thought you were one of the partners at—"

"I am. But Carson started the company. He's in charge."

"That's why you follow his orders?"

Tanner shrugged. "He's a good leader most of the time. If I didn't think that of him, there's not a damn thing he could make me do. I respect him."

"Enough to marry a stranger, it seems." Blair tucked a curl behind her ear. "I don't know if I thanked you for that, by the way. Marrying me, I mean. I know you didn't want to."

Tanner set his mug down, taking a step toward her. "I didn't."

Blair's pulse quickened, but she didn't back away. "Well, hopefully it will all be over soon, right?"

"Right." He moved closer, close enough that she had to tilt her head back to maintain eye contact.

"And then we can go our separate ways."

"Right."

"And you'll never have to see me again." She wasn't sure what she was fishing for. Maybe a compliment. Maybe some sort of reassurance that she wasn't the only one struggling with a strange physical attraction.

Before Tanner said anything, his phone chimed. He checked it, and huffed out what might've been considered a chuckle. At least for him.

"Benedict," he explained. "He got you approved for lab access. Tomorrow morning. It's in a secure facility."

All of the tension from before evaporated as Blair bounced on her toes, a wide grin on her face. "I can work in an actual lab? With equipment? Not just remote access?"

"Limited capacity. Full security protocols. But yes." The corner of Tanner's mouth twitched upward. "A real lab."

Blair's entire system flooded with endorphins. Without conscious thought, her body reacted before her mind could process—she launched herself at Tanner, arms wrapping around him in a spontaneous embrace.

"Thank you!" The words tumbled out, riding a wave of pure biochemical euphoria. "This is wonderful. I can test the protein marker bonding rates in real time. I can verify the myelin regeneration pathway. I can actually see if the C4-C7 results replicate under controlled conditions. This changes everything!"

She stopped abruptly. Oh shit. She was pressed against Tanner, arms around his neck, body practically vibrating with excitement. Tanner had gone completely still, his muscles rigid beneath her touch.

"Sorry," she said, starting to pull away. "I got excited and my limbic system overrode my frontal lobe control. Another classic amygdala hijack. I didn't mean to invade your personal space."

His arms came around her, holding her in place. "Don't apologize."

The embrace shifted from awkward to something else. Blair relaxed against him, allowing herself to absorb the comfort of human contact after weeks of isolation and fear.

His heartbeat pounded against her cheek, steady and strong, albeit a bit faster than the average adult male. His arms encircled her completely. He was a fortified wall against the world around her. More secure than any reinforced safe house.

When they finally separated, Blair cleared her throat. "I should review the data. Prepare for tomorrow and all that fun stuff. I need to optimize my testing priorities."

Tanner nodded, stepping back. "I'll handle security arrangements."

As she turned to go, he spoke again. "Blair."

She paused, looking back at him.

"You did well today."

The simple praise shouldn't have triggered such a profound dopamine response. But coming from him—from this man of few words and fewer compliments—it felt like winning a Nobel Prize.

"Thank you," she said, offering him a small smile.

CHAPTER SIX

TANNER

A WHOLE MOTHERFUCKING MONTH OF MARRIAGE, AND Tanner still hadn't figured out how to stop cataloging every detail about his wife. The way she tucked her hair behind her ear when concentrating. The barely audible hum she made when analyzing data. The angle of her shoulders when she was onto something promising. The soft exhale when a test yielded expected results.

Irrelevant details for mission parameters. Essential data for the growing complication that was his reaction to her.

Tanner leaned against the lab wall, arms crossed, tracking Blair's movements without seeming to. The slow tap of her fingers on the keyboard. The flex of her wrist when she adjusted the microscope. His pulse kicked up when she bit her lower lip.

Six nights now. Six goddamn nights waking up hard and aching, blankets twisted from dreams that left his skin too tight. Visions of pressing her against the lab table, tasting the hum in her throat. Teeth biting into her thigh. Her fingernails scratching up his back.

And now? His body didn't give a shit about mission boundaries. Not with the way her blouse gaped when she leaned forward, not with the scent of her rosemary shampoo clinging to the air. Tanner exhaled through his nose, forcing his focus to the security feeds.

"Something wrong?" Blair's voice cut through his thoughts.

Tanner met her gaze. "No." An automatic lie.

Her eyes narrowed, that sharp mind dissecting him. If she knew—if she ever realized exactly what kind of threat he was becoming—she'd bolt. And he wouldn't blame her.

With great effort, Tanner forced his attention away from her. He maintained a line of sight on all entry points while Blair worked. The two weeks of lab access had transformed her. The defeated woman from their first meeting had been replaced by a focused scientist in her element—confident, precise, occasionally muttering complex terminology to herself that he understood only because his sister had the same habit. Well, that and he'd spent the nights where he'd woken up with an erection researching neurochemistry while she slept so that he wouldn't have to face the reoccurring thoughts of Blair naked and moaning on top of him.

Besides, it was wise to know his asset's work to better protect it. And her.

That's what he told himself anyway.

The lab smelled of antiseptic and coffee, the low hum of centrifuges and refrigeration units creating a white noise backdrop that reminded him of forward operating bases—the constant mechanical sounds that eventually became so familiar you only noticed when they stopped. The secure facility occupied the sublevel of a private research building owned by a Crest Strategies client. Three biometric checkpoints between the entrance and this room. Limited personnel. Sixteen security cameras with a four-second blind spot at the southeast corner that he'd already reported and had scheduled for correction.

Not ideal, but workable. Tanner had memorized the building schematics, identified exit routes, mapped potential choke points, and established defensive positions in case of a hostile breach. The weight of his Glock against his ribs was a constant reassurance.

His phone vibrated with an encrypted message. He checked it without taking his eyes off Blair, who was pipetting something with absolute concentration, her lower lip caught between her teeth. The sight triggered an unwarranted spike in his heart rate that he immediately suppressed.

> I have something. Meet secure channel 0900.
> – Major L

Tanner's jaw tightened. Derek Lawson had been his commanding officer before Kandahar, before the intelligence failure that had cost multiple civilian lives. Now, Lawson worked intelligence for a private military contractor and occasionally provided information when Tanner needed it.

"Good news?" Blair asked without looking up from her microscope.

Tanner glanced at his watch. 0842. "Potentially. I need to step out briefly."

She made a humming sound that he'd learned meant acknowledgment. He'd also learned that when she was deep in research mode, she became remarkably concise, as if conserving words for her mental calculations.

"Want me to stay here?" She asked, finally looking up. The overhead lights caught the flecks in her hazel eyes, another detail he had no reason to notice.

"Yes. Lock the door. No personnel entry without my voice confirmation."

Blair nodded, already returning to her work. "How long?"

"Fifteen minutes max."

He slipped into the corridor, moving to a secured communication room they'd established on arrival. Inside, he activated the encrypted video link precisely at 0900, years of military punctuality making even one-minute deviations unacceptable.

Major Derek Lawson's face appeared on screen, new creases around his eyes since Tanner had last seen him in person. Afghanistan had aged them all differently; some in the face, some in the soul.

"Whitney," Lawson acknowledged. "You still look like you eat nails for breakfast."

"You have information?" Tanner kept his voice neutral, ignoring the attempt at camaraderie.

Lawson's expression sobered. "Direct as ever. I've confirmed your companies suspicions about a Dr. Collin Asicks. The whistleblower report didn't originate from a concerned colleague. Asicks was hired by Nexus Biometrics six weeks before he filed the report."

Tanner's mind processed the confirmation. Nexus Biometrics was a major defense contractor specializing in neural interface technology. Their headquarters occupied a glass tower in Northern Virginia, fifteen minutes from the Pentagon. Most of their primary contracts were with DARPA, the Naval Research Laboratory, and three classified intelligence agencies. They were a competitor in Blair's research field. The company had been on Carson's suspect list, but confirmation was valuable.

"Evidence?"

"Financial transfers through three shell companies. Eventually landed in an account in Asicks' wife's maiden name. Amateur mistake." Lawson tapped something on his keyboard. "Sending the transaction records now. Even tried to obscure it through cryptocurrency conversion, but left digital fingerprints all over the blockchain."

"Motive beyond acquisition?"

"That's where it gets interesting." Lawson leaned closer to the camera, the movement causing his image to pixelate momentarily. "Nexus has a neural regeneration project that's been stuck in pre-clinical for two years. Significant investment, minimal results. Their approach uses ion channel manipulation instead of myelin reconstruction—fundamentally flawed methodology. Your Dr. Winters's breakthrough would render their approach obsolete."

Tanner nodded, refraining from correcting Lawson about Blair's last name. Corporate sabotage. Strategic elimination of competition. "Are there other players involved?"

"Nexus is prime. But they've got government connections—Defense Advanced Research Projects Agency contracts, intelligence community consulting. They can make problems disappear."

Or people. Like they'd tried to do with Annabelle.

"I'm sending you a name. Someone to be wary of. Dominic Penten. He's tight with the head of Nexus security operations. A contractor. Former JSOC, dishonorable discharge. Suspected involvement in three corporate extractions in the last eighteen months. We served together briefly in Helmand Province. Cold operator, efficient, no ethical boundaries."

Extraction. Military euphemism for kidnapping. Tanner's hand tightened around the pencil he'd been holding, the wood cracking under pressure. The sound echoed in the small room.

"How's the surveillance on Dr. Winters?" Lawson asked.

"It's comprehensive," Tanner replied. "Multiple layers, redundant systems, constant monitoring."

"Smart. Penten doesn't give up easily. If he's been tasked with acquiring her and her research..." Lawson let the implication hang.

"Understood. Anything else?"

"Just watch your six, Whitney. These corporate operations can get messy fast. Penten operates with private sector resources. Makes him unpredictable."

The call ended, and Tanner tossed the broken pencil onto a nearby table. Nexus Biometrics. Dominic Penten. Concrete targets rather than abstract threats. He should feel satisfied. Instead, unease crawled up his spine.

The confirmation of an external threat changed things. His initial mission—Carson's plan to control Blair's research through their arranged marriage—was being superseded by a more immediate objective: protecting her from a very real danger.

Protecting her, not just her research.

Tanner returned to the lab, finding Blair exactly where he'd left her, though she'd moved to computer analysis of whatever she'd been examining. The blue light from the monitor reflected on her face, and damn if she wasn't beautiful. Fucking damn it.

"Everything okay?" she asked, glancing up briefly.

"Yes and no. I received confirmed intel. The whistleblower, Dr. Asicks, was hired by Nexus Biometrics." Blair's fingers froze over the keyboard. "Asicks? That backstabbing son of a—" She caught herself, taking a deep breath. "I knew something was off with his claims. The molecular structures he cited couldn't possibly have been interpreted as having weapons applications without deliberate misrepresentation. He specifically omitted the quaternary protein structure that prevents systemic binding."

"Corporate sabotage. Competitor elimination."

"Nexus." Blair's expression hardened. "They've been trying to duplicate my approach for years. Their neural regeneration project uses a completely different pathway—ion channel manipulation rather than myelin reconstruction. They're trying to force potassium-sodium ion exchange to stimulate neural regrowth, but it creates systemic inflammatory responses and cascading cytokine problems. I've told them repeatedly at conferences that they're wasting their time and research subjects."

Tanner raised an eyebrow, trying to decide if he needed to ask for a more simple description in layman's terms, but decided against it. "I need to brief Carson. There may be security implications."

Blair nodded, already turning back to her work. "When do we leave?"

"Three hours."

"Perfect." She was already lost in her research again, that remarkable focus descending like a shield around her.

Tanner resumed his position, sending a brief encrypted message to Carson and Benedict about the Nexus confirmation. His phone buzzed almost immediately with Carson's response:

> Use this. Gala tonight at Biltmore. Scientific innovation fundraiser. Key research community members present. Opportunity to neutralize Nexus influence.

Followed by Benedict's more detailed assessment.

> The security risks at the event are significant
> but manageable. Plus, the reputation benefits
> could be substantial. Blair's interview created
> an opening for reintroduction to the scientific
> community. Nexus representatives will likely
> be present.

Tanner's jaw clenched. A public appearance meant exposure. Exposure meant vulnerability. Vulnerability meant risk.

Yet they weren't wrong about the strategic advantage. Blair's reputation rehabilitation had momentum after the interview. The scientific community was beginning to question the bioweapon narrative. Confronting the situation directly, with knowledge of who was behind it, had merit.

He typed a reply, then sent a detailed request to Jenna Briggs, the head of security at Crest Strategies

> Briggs, get details about event tonight from
> Crest. I've approved maximum security
> protocols. Full team deployment. Advance site
> inspection required. Minimum three egress
> routes confirmed before arrival. Vehicle
> positions at all exits.

He glanced at Blair, who was completely absorbed in her work. They'd been living in a bubble of relative safety at Location Charlie and the secure lab. Tonight would thrust them into public view.

As a married couple.

Ah, shit.

———

BACK AT LOCATION CHARLIE, TANNER IMPLEMENTED security preparations while Blair showered and changed. He verified team positions for the evening, established extraction protocols, and mapped the Biltmore Hotel's layout, identifying choke points and defensive positions. Twenty-three minutes spent checking weapons and tactical gear. Seventeen minutes coordinating with Benedict on communication channels and code words.

All standard procedures for high-risk operations.

What wasn't standard was the uncomfortable awareness that kept intruding—the sound of Blair moving in the bedroom, the anticipation of seeing her dressed formally, the memory of her spontaneous embrace when lab access had been approved. Distractions he couldn't afford but couldn't seem to eliminate.

When Blair emerged from her room in comfortable clothes, her hair still damp from the shower, Tanner was reviewing satellite imagery of the Biltmore's surrounding streets. She curled up on the couch with her tablet, the golden afternoon light streaming through bulletproof windows illuminating her profile.

"Can't stop thinking about the lab results," she explained without looking up. "The new protein marker configuration is showing 82% efficacy in vitro. That's a 4% improvement over previous trials. If I can stabilize the tertiary structure during synthesis, we might push it to 85%."

Tanner nodded. "Delivery arrived," he said, gesturing to the garment bags hanging on the coat rack.

Blair glanced up, then set aside her tablet with a sigh. "I suppose I should start getting ready. Women are expected to take hours for these things, right?"

"I guess. I have limited experience with formal event preparation protocols, except when it comes to the security for then."

That earned him another laugh, the sound lightening something in his chest. "Of course. I bet you can be combat-ready in under three minutes."

"Two minutes, seventeen seconds. Full tactical gear and primary weapons. Three minutes, forty-two seconds with complete kit and secondary armaments."

"Impressive. You seem to be fast at everything."

He bit his lip and raised an eyebrow at her. "Not everything, Doctor."

Her cheeks flushed as she stood, avoiding his gaze. "Right, well,

I'll just..." She turned, then paused. With a deep breath, she stretched in a way that momentarily distracted him; her arms overhead, back arching, the hem of her shirt rising to reveal a strip of skin above her jeans. "I'll need at least an hour. Maybe two. I haven't done formal hair and makeup myself in ages."

Tanner watched her take the garment bag labeled with her name and disappear into her bedroom. While she was in there, he changed into the tuxedo Benedict had arranged, the formal wear tailored to conceal his weapons while allowing full range of motion if combat became necessary. The weight of the shoulder holster against his ribs was familiar, reassuring. He was adjusting his cufflinks when Blair's bedroom door opened.

Every system in his brain short-circuited.

"Fuck," he breathed out.

Blair wore a deep jade gown that left one shoulder bare, the fabric clinging to curves before flowing to the floor. Her dark curls were swept up, exposing the elegant line of her neck and the delicate architecture of her collarbones. Diamond studs caught the light when she moved, drawing his attention to the curve of her ears. The gown's color intensified the green in her hazel eyes, making them appear almost luminous in the room's soft lighting.

His mouth went dry, his pulse sped up, and for 3.7 seconds, he forgot to breathe.

"Do I look okay?" she asked, misinterpreting his silence.

"Yes." The word came out half choked.

Blair smiled, a hint of uncertainty in her eyes. "You clean up pretty well yourself."

Tanner inclined his head, acknowledging the compliment while trying to regain focus. The dress was more than pleasing—it was strategically effective. Blair looked confident, successful, completely opposite from someone whose career was in shambles. It projected exactly the image they needed for tonight.

That she looked stunning enough to momentarily disable his combat readiness was irrelevant.

"Oh," Blair said, fumbling with something in her hand. "Benedict sent this. Said it was important for maintaining our cover." She held up a delicate necklace with a small diamond pendant. "But I can't get the clasp. Could you...?"

Tanner crossed to her, taking the necklace from her outstretched hand. Blair turned, presenting her back to him, and swept a few stray curls aside. The gesture exposed the nape of her neck, vulnerable and trusting in a way that triggered both protective instincts and something far less honorable.

His hands, capable of disassembling a Barrett M82 sniper rifle in complete darkness, suddenly felt clumsy. The delicate chain seemed impossibly small between his fingers, which had ended lives with less effort than it now took to work the tiny clasp. He forced himself to focus, to ignore the scent of her perfume.

The clasp finally secured, but Tanner lingered. His fingers brushed against her skin as he adjusted the chain, a fleeting contact that sent awareness cascading through his system.

Blair turned, now standing close enough that he could see the individual gold flecks in her hazel eyes, the slight unevenness in her lipstick application, the nearly imperceptible scar at her temple partially concealed by makeup. "Thank you."

Tanner stepped back. "You look..." His words trailed off.

"Decent?" She suggested.

He shook his head. "Perfect."

———

THE BILTMORE HOTEL'S GRAND BALLROOM GLITTERED WITH crystal chandeliers. Tanner's team had switched the hotel's security with their own personnel. Penn had hacked into the hotel's security system, giving them access to all camera feeds.

As they entered, Tanner conducted an automatic threat assessment. Three main exits. Four service corridors. There were approximately 400 attendees. Staff circulated with champagne and hors d'oeuvres. A small orchestra played in the corner—the violin case could potentially conceal a disassembled weapon, though the elderly musician showed no indicators of operative training.

"Stop counting exit routes and potential weapons," Blair murmured beside him. "You're making your murder face."

Tanner relaxed his expression. "Standard security protocol."

"Well, your standard security protocol looks like you're planning an assassination." She slipped her hand into the crook of his arm, her fingers applying gentle pressure. "We're supposed to be a happily married couple, remember? Try to look less like you're about to snap someone's neck."

Tanner adjusted, placing his hand over hers in what he hoped appeared to be an affectionate gesture. The warmth of her skin against his sent an irrational surge of calm through his system.

"Better," Blair said, her voice carrying a hint of amusement. "Now, let's go. I see at least three department chairs I need to speak with."

For the next hour, Tanner remained vigilant while Blair navigated the scientific community. She addressed the bioweapon allegations directly but briefly, then pivoted to discussing her current research in terms that clearly captivated her colleagues. Several expressed skepticism about the whistleblower's claims, particularly after Blair explained the molecular structures in terms Tanner only partially understood despite his recent research.

Throughout, she maintained physical contact with him—a hand on his arm, shoulders brushing, small touches that established their relationship without overt displays. The vanilla scent of her perfume mingled with the champagne on her breath when she leaned close to whisper observations about various scientists in the room.

"Blair!" A gray-haired man approached. "I was hoping you'd be here. Your interview was illuminating."

"Dr. Kustka," Blair greeted him with a genuine smile. "Thank you for your public statement questioning the allegations. It meant a great deal."

"Nonsense. Anyone who actually understands molecular neurobiology could see the whistleblower report was fundamentally flawed. The claimed chemical pathway would have required ignoring basic principles of protein binding." The older scientist turned to Tanner with an assessing gaze that reminded him of senior officers. "And you must be the husband I've heard about."

"Tanner Whitney," he confirmed, offering his hand, noting the doctor's firm grip despite age-related joint inflammation.

"Someone mentioned you were from a security background," Dr. Kustka said. "Though he implied it was more corporate than...whatever you actually are."

Tanner remained expressionless. "Security consultant."

"Hmm." Dr. Kustka's eyes twinkled. "Well, Blair certainly needs good protection these days. Especially with Nexus representatives here tonight."

Blair tensed beside him, her fingers tightening almost imperceptibly on his arm. "They're here?"

"Oh yes. Dr. Hannibel and his associate, Mr. Penten, are by the bar. They've been watching you since you arrived."

Tanner stiffened.

"Thank you for the warning," Blair said, her voice steady despite the slight increase in her pulse where Tanner's fingers rested against her wrist.

"Just be careful," Dr. Kustka advised. "Academic competition is one thing. Corporate espionage is quite another."

As the scientist moved away, Blair turned to Tanner. "Penten. That's the name you mentioned, isn't it?"

"Yes. Former Joint Special Operations Command. Dishonorable discharge." Tanner kept his voice low, positioning himself to block lip-reading surveillance techniques. "Now Nexus bull dog they use for less sightly activities."

"What do you think he's doing here?"

"Surveillance, possibly more."

Blair's grip on his arm tightened. "More meaning...?"

"It's a decent extraction opportunity."

She paled, the makeup on her cheeks suddenly more apparent against her skin. "You think they'd try something here? With hundreds of witnesses?"

"It's unlikely, but be prepared for anything."

Blair took a deep breath, squaring her shoulders with the same determination he'd seen earlier. "Well, I'm not hiding in the corner all night. In fact, I think it's time to be proactive."

Before Tanner could stop her, she was moving across the room toward Penten and an older gentleman, pulling Tanner along with her. He adjusted immediately, positioning himself ahead of her, prepared to intercept any threat. His right hand moved closer to his concealed weapon, muscle memory taking over.

Part of him wanted to shut this down immediately. Public confrontation increased risk profiles exponentially. But another part— the part that had spent weeks cataloging Blair's determination and resilience—felt a reluctant admiration for her refusal to be intimidated.

"Dr. Hannibel, Mr. Penten," Blair greeted them. "I understand you're representing Nexus Biometrics tonight. I'm Dr. Blair Whitney. I believe your company has taken quite an interest in my research recently."

Penten's expression remained neutral, but Tanner didn't miss the flash of surprise in his eyes. This confrontation had clearly caught him off guard too.

"Dr. Whitney," Dr. Hannibel responded smoothly, offering his hand, which Blair shook. "Your reputation precedes you."

"Yes, I imagine it does, given how hard your company is working to steal it."

Dr. Hannibel's perfect smile faltered, the right corner dropping a fraction a second before the left. "I'm not sure what you're implying."

"I think you know exactly what I'm implying." Blair's voice remained conversational. "Dr. Asicks didn't develop concerns about my research on his own."

Dominic Penten straightened, his posture shifting. Tanner mirrored the movement, preparing for potential escalation, cataloging the nearest weapons and barriers should the situation deteriorate.

"That's quite an accusation," Dr. Hannibel said, his smile now completely gone. "One that could be considered defamatory without evidence."

"Evidence exists," Tanner interjected, his voice pitched low enough that only their small group could hear. "As does documentation of Nexus's failed neural regeneration project. Interesting timing, your whistleblower appearing just as Dr. Whitney's research succeeded where yours failed."

Penten's eyes narrowed at Tanner. "And you must be her new husband. Mr. Whitney, I presume? Strange timing for a wedding, I'll admit."

"Well, my wife and I decided not to let life get in the way of our relationship," Tanner said, lifting his chin. It was a challenge to Penten, to see if he'd question the legality of the marriage. He didn't.

"Congratulations, I suppose. If you'll excuse us, we have people to see." Penten stood, guiding Dr. Hannibel away.

"That was either very brave or very stupid," Tanner said quietly as he led Blair in the opposite direction with hand resting on her lower back.

"Maybe both," she admitted. "But I'm tired of being reactive. Tired of waiting for them to make the next move."

"Understood. But still..."

Blair nodded. "I know. It felt good, though, to see their faces when they realized we know what they did."

For the next hour, they continued circulating, though Tanner noticed Blair's energy flagging. The orchestra had transitioned to slower pieces, and several couples moved to the dance floor. Maintaining their cover as a married couple would normally dictate participation, but Tanner hesitated, unwilling to compromise his surveillance position.

Blair solved the dilemma by swaying in time with the music, her body moving closer to his. "We should probably dance at least once," she murmured. "For appearance's sake."

Tanner assessed the dance floor—limited cover, compromised sightlines, reduced mobility. But refusing would draw more attention than accepting.

"Fine," he said, guiding her toward the edge of the dance floor where he could maintain visual contact with both exits and Penten's position.

He placed one hand at the small of her back, the other taking her hand in a formal dance position. Blair moved into his space with surprising grace, her body fitting against his.

"I'm surprised you know how to dance," she said as they began moving to the music.

"Standard training. Undercover operations often include social functions."

Blair laughed softly, the sound vibrating against his chest where they touched. "Of course. Military dancecraft. I should have known."

They moved together; her following his lead as if they'd rehearsed. Tanner kept Penten in his peripheral vision at all times, noting when the man spoke quietly into what appeared to be a communication device disguised as a cufflink. Three new individuals entered the ballroom within two minutes of each other—all male, all with the distinctive posture of security personnel, all moving to positions around the perimeter.

"Something's happening," Tanner murmured to Blair. "Prepare to leave."

"What? Where?" Her eyes widened, pupils dilating as she stared up at him.

"Penten activated additional personnel. Three new security-trained individuals entered within the last five minutes."

Blair glanced around, trying to spot what he'd observed. "Should we leave?"

"Soon. Stay calm. We'll leave through the east exit in three minutes."

She nodded, continuing their dance without missing a beat. Tanner was impressed by her composure, the way she showed no outward sign of alarm despite the tension he could feel in her body where it pressed against his.

Two minutes later, Tanner noted Penten moving toward the east exit. "Damn it. Change of plan. West service corridor. Take my hand and keep smiling. It's best if they don't know we know."

Despite the fear written in her eyes, she flashed him a grin and slipped her hand into his outstretched one. She allowed Tanner to guide her toward the kitchens. They had almost reached the service door when Tanner spotted one of Penten's men intercepting their path.

"Bathroom," Tanner directed, altering course again.

They reached the hallway leading to the restrooms, momentarily out of sight of the main ballroom. The corridor smelled of cleaning products and expensive hand soap, the lighting dimmer than the ballroom's crystal-refracted brilliance. Blair's breathing had accelerated, but she maintained her composure better than Tanner had expected.

"Go into the women's restroom," Tanner instructed. "Wait thirty seconds. Exit and turn left. There's a service elevator at the end of the hall. I'll meet you there."

"What are you going to do?"

"Someone needs a nap. Go."

Blair hesitated only briefly before following his instructions. The moment she disappeared into the restroom, Tanner positioned himself in a blind spot near the hallway entrance, controlling his breathing. The weight of the Glock against his ribs was reassuring.

He didn't wait long. The man appeared, striding directly towards the women's restroom. He paused, reaching into his inside left coat pocket where a flash of metal reflected.

Tanner moved silently behind him. His arm locked around the operative's throat in a lateral vascular neck restraint, compressing the carotid arteries while applying pressure to prevent vocalization. The technique—perfected during close-quarters combat training—restricted blood flow to the brain without affecting the airway. The man struggled briefly, hand moving toward his concealed weapon, before losing consciousness. The entire encounter lasted less than twelve seconds.

Tanner lowered the unconscious man into a nearby utility closet, securing him with military-grade zip ties from his concealed pocket.

The operative would be discovered eventually, but not before they were long gone.

Moving to the service elevator, Tanner arrived just as Blair emerged from the restroom.

"Fuck!" Blair whisper-yelled, placing a hand over her heart. "You scared the shit out of me."

"Let's go." Then into his concealed microphone, he said, "Emergency exit protocol initiated. Service exit. Vehicle three. Potential pursuit."

Jenna Brigg's voice came through his earpiece. "Understood. The vehicle is in position. The second team is creating a distraction at the main entrance. Go now."

The service elevator opened into the hotel's back service area. Tanner led Blair through the kitchen, past startled staff, and out to a loading dock where a black SUV waited, engine running.

He helped her into the vehicle, then slid behind the wheel. Before Blair could speak, he was driving, taking them away from the hotel.

"What happened back there?" she finally asked as they merged onto the highway, the SUV's engine humming.

"Penten deployed operatives to kidnap you."

"Fuck!"

"My thought exactly." Tanner checked the mirrors, looking for pursuit. "I put one down. There are potentially others following."

Blair twisted in her seat, looking behind them. "I don't see anyone."

"Still... Hold on." He took a sudden exit, then an immediate turn onto a side street, the tires protesting at the sharp maneuver.

For the next twenty minutes, Tanner implemented evasive driving techniques—sudden turns, doubling back, using parking structures to change direction unseen. Blair remained silent beside him, her knuckles white where she gripped the door handle, her controlled breathing betraying her effort to remain calm.

Finally, they reached a small garage where another vehicle waited. Tanner performed a final sweep for surveillance before transferring them to the second car—a nondescript sedan with reinforced door panels and bulletproof glass that would attract no attention in regular traffic.

"Are we safe now?" Blair asked as they pulled back onto the road, the sound of rain beginning to patter against the windshield.

"For now."

She nodded, her breathing gradually slowing. "Thank you. For getting us out of there."

Tanner glanced at her. The elegant updo had partly collapsed, curls escaping around her face. The jade dress was slightly rumpled from their hasty exit. A small run had developed in her stockings near her ankle.

"It's my job," he said, though both knew it was more than that.

"We're not going back to Location Charlie, are we?" she finally asked, staring out the window.

"Too risky. We'll go to a secondary safe location for tonight and return to Charlie after a security sweep tomorrow."

"Where are we going?"

"A hotel. Secure reservation. Different name. Prepaid with cash. Level 3 security protocols."

Blair nodded, accepting this change without further question.

They reached the hotel; a mid-range chain with decent security features: limited access points, functioning door alarms, non-networked key card systems, and minimal surveillance cameras in public areas only. Tanner had selected it specifically for these attributes, not for convenience. He checked them in using one of his established cover identities, guiding Blair through a side entrance to avoid the lobby.

The room was standard. A king bed, basic furniture, unremarkable décor. But it offered three critical security advantages: corner position minimizing shared walls, direct fire escape access, and reinforced door with secondary locking mechanism Tanner had installed during previous operations. He performed a comprehensive security sweep while Blair stood in the center of the room, still in her evening gown, looking somewhat lost.

"It's clear," he announced, holstering his weapon. "The perimeter is secure."

Blair nodded, then suddenly her composure cracked. Her hands began to shake, her breathing becoming rapid and shallow.

"They were really going to take me," she said, her voice unsteady. "Right there, in the middle of a gala with hundreds of witnesses."

Tanner moved toward her. "Yes."

"If you hadn't been there, if you hadn't noticed..."

"But I was and I did." He reached for her hands, steadying them in his larger ones. Her skin felt cold. "You're safe."

Her eyes met his, pupils dilated with residual fear and adrenaline. "For how long, Tanner? How long before they try again? Before they succeed?"

"They won't succeed."

"You can't know that." Her voice cracked. "You can't be with me every second of every day until this is over. What if it takes the rest of my life?"

"I will protect you. Protecting you is my mission."

"Your mission," she repeated, something shifting in her expression —a mixture of disappointment and resignation. "Right. I'm just your 24/7 babysitting job."

"No," he corrected. "That's not true."

"Yes it is. I'm just an assignment."

"No, you're not." He tilted her chin and forced her to look at him. "You're my wife."

Blair's breath caught. Her gaze searched his face, looking for something Tanner wasn't sure how to give. The vulnerability in her expression triggered his protective instincts while simultaneously threatening his emotional defenses.

Then she moved, closing the distance between them, and pressed her lips to his.

CHAPTER SEVEN

BLAIR

FOR ONE LONG SECOND, BLAIR WONDERED IF SHE'D JUST made the biggest mistake of her life. Tanner froze against her. Didn't return the kiss. Didn't move to hold her. He just… froze.

Blair's stomach dropped. She pulled back, her pulse hammering. "Shit. I shouldn't have—"

Tanner's hand tangled in her hair, dragging her mouth back to his. The brutal kiss was hungry; nothing like the tentative brush of lips she'd initiated. His other arm hooked under her thighs, easily lifting her against him as her dress bunched around her waist. She gasped into his mouth, legs locking around his hips, heels digging into the back of his legs.

The room blurred. Tanner's grip was iron, his demanding mouth hot against hers. He walked them backward until her spine hit the wall, pinning her there with his hips. His teeth scraped her lower lip, and she moaned, fingers tearing at his jacket.

"Off," she panted against his mouth. "Get these fucking clothes off."

Tanner didn't hesitate. His hands were everywhere; peeling fabric, dragging zippers, snapping buttons. Her dress pooled at her feet, his jacket and shirt following. The air hit her bare skin, and his body was hotter, his hands rougher than she'd imagined. And the tattoos... They were everywhere. Up his torso, around his ribs, encircling those tree-trunk arms. The ink traveled over his shoulders, curling up his neck. He was a walking art exhibit, and if she hadn't been so consumed with the fire burning in her lower belly, she would've taken the time to appreciate them.

But she'd almost just been kidnapped, and life was too fucking short. She reached for his belt, fumbling with the buckle. Tanner swore under his breath, catching her wrist.

"Slow down," he growled.

"I don't want slow."

His thumb pressed against her pulse point, his voice dark. "Blair. Slow. Down."

Tanner dragged her to the bed, pushing her onto the mattress. His eyes raked over her; lingerie still intact, stockings clinging to her thighs. He knelt between her legs, fingers tracing the lace edge of her panties. "Fuck, you're gorgeous."

She arched into his touch, but he pulled back, smirking.

"Patience."

Her ex had never looked at her like this. God, he'd been too busy with his own release. Half the time, it'd hurt like hell because she hadn't been ready. Shit. What if her current husband was the same?

But no. Tanner stared at her like she was something to savor. Her ex had taken what he wanted and left her hollow. But Tanner's hands were relentless, his mouth trailing down her stomach, lower, lower—

She gasped when his tongue flicked over her clit through the lace. "Tanner—"

He hooked his fingers in the fabric, tearing it away. The sound ripped through her, her hips jerking off the bed.

"Fuck," he growled against her thigh. "You're wet."

He was right. Damn. She couldn't remember the last time she'd been this ready.

His mouth was on her before she could reply. Hot, wet, relentless. His tongue circled her clit, then plunged inside, fucking her with slow strokes. Blair's fingers twisted in the sheets, her breath coming in ragged bursts.

"Look at me," he ordered.

She forced her eyes open. Tanner's gaze burned into hers as he sucked her clit between his teeth, and with a steady push, he slid one finger and then a second into her. Holy fucking shit. Just two of his fingers had filled her more than she had been in ages. And, fuck if his hands weren't massive.

He curled his fingers inside her, watching her with his dark eyes. The sight alone sent her crashing over the edge. She came with a cry, her thighs clamping around his head.

Tanner didn't let up. He licked her through it, drawing out every shudder, every gasp. When she finally collapsed back, boneless, he crawled up her body; he'd already removed the rest of his clothes. His cock pressed against her thigh; thick, hard, bigger than she'd expected.

There was no way in fucking hell that massive thing was going to fit inside her. No fucking way. Not without a lot of pain.

"You clean?" He asked, drawing her attention to his face, but only for a moment before her wide-eyed gaze dropped back down to the python resting against her.

"STI-free." She hesitated. "I'm... sterile."

His brow furrowed, but he didn't push as to why. He didn't prod until she told him that she'd been terrified of bringing her abusive husband's children into the world that she'd gone to extreme measures behind his back. That he'd beaten her within an inch of her life when he'd found out. Tanner just nodded. "Me too, on both accounts."

Something warm swelled within Blair, and she reached for his dick, but he caught her wrist again. "No. We need to go slow. I don't want to hurt... we need lube."

"What?" Blair's brows furrowed. "Why?"

"Because you're fucking tight and I'm fucking huge. And I am not going to hurt you." He sat back on his heels, glancing around the room.

"You won't—"

"Yes I will. It's happened before."

Blair didn't want to think about the fact that he'd been with other women when she was about to fuck him. "I doubt there's any lube here."

"Fuck." Tanner ran a hand through his short hair. A second later, he swore again, dragging a hand down his face. "We need lube."

"There *isn't* any."

"There *should* be." His frustration wrinkled his forehead. It was almost cute, though she doubted he'd want to hear that.

Again, Blair's attention dropped to that gorgeous, enormous dick.

"What are you—fucking hell, Blair," he hissed.

Blair grabbed the base of Tanner's cock, stroking him once, twice—her fingers barely meeting around his girth. "I don't care about lube." She said, staring up at him through her eyelashes. "Just fuck me."

Tanner's jaw tightened even as he watched her stroke him. "No."

"I can take it."

"Bullshit." His hand closed over hers, stilling her movements. "I felt how tight you were when I had my fingers in you. You'll tear."

She didn't back down. "So I'll tear. It wouldn't be the first time." Again, her mind went to her ex.

A muscle in Tanner's throat jumped, and darkness crossed his face. He wasn't an idiot. He likely knew why she'd been hurt during sex before. Or maybe that darkness was the same lust she felt.

Blair hooked her ankle behind his knee. "Improvise."

His gaze dropped between her legs, then snapped back to her face. "Improvise?"

"Either fuck me..." She wasn't used to explaining herself, least of all like this. "Or get me wetter."

For a second, she thought he'd give in—his control was fraying, his breathing ragged. But then he swore and dragged her up, flipping her onto her stomach before she could protest.

"I said *slow*." His grip on her hips was bruising as he pulled her to her knees, spreading them wider until she was bare and prone before him.

Blair shivered at the command in his voice. She heard him spit, and then his slick fingers slipped between her thighs, gliding over her soaked folds, testing.

"Still not enough," he growled.

She went to argue, but his fingers curled inside her again. He was not as gentle as he had been before. And maybe he was right because just the stretch of his two fingers burned. But it wasn't too painful. It helped that he used the combination of the heel of his palm on her clit and his fingers stroking the spot that made her gasp. His other hand tangled in her hair, forcing her head down against the sheets.

"Stay."

His mouth replaced his fingers, tongue circling her clit, then plunging deeper, fucking her with slow, filthy strokes. She couldn't move, couldn't think beyond the heat coiling low in her stomach. When she came the second time, it wrecked her, her thighs shook, her nails ripped the sheets.

Tanner didn't stop.

Her third orgasm hit harder, wrenched from her with a sob as his fingers crooked inside her, working in time with his mouth. She was drenched, oversensitive, her whole body strung tight.

"Now," she gasped, pushing up on trembling arms. "Now."

Tanner's breath was hot against her thigh. "Fine. But you're going to ride me. You control how much you take." He switched spots with her, lying on his back. Tanner moved between her legs, his cock jutting against her. Goddamn, she couldn't even wrap her hand all the way around it.

Blair swallowed.

Tanner didn't give her time to think. He dragged her up, positioning her straddled above him. "Slow."

She sank down, inch by slow inch, her breath hitching as she stretched around him. The burn was immediate. Her thighs trembled.

"Shit, Tanner," she moaned.

"Fuck," Tanner gritted out, hands flexing on her waist. His neck was corded with tension. "You're so tight, Blair. *Jesus.*"

She took more. Too much. She whimpered.

"Stop." His voice was gravel. "Fucking—stop. Don't move."

She froze, breathing hard.

Tanner swore under his breath, his thumbs circling her hip bones. "You okay?"

She nodded. "Just… give me a second."

"Take all the seconds you need."

The pain was there, an insistent ache, but beneath it was something else—sharp pleasure. She rolled her hips experimentally, and his head tipped back with a groan.

"Christ. Fucking hell. Don't do that unless you want this over fast."

A laugh startled out of her.

His eyes darkened. "I'm serious, Blair."

Blair rolled her hips—just a little—and his cock dragged inside her, hitting deeper. She gasped. Tanner cursed, his grip tightening.

"Are you?" she asked, raising an eyebrow.

"Yes. Fuck yes."

But she was already moving, finding her rhythm. The stretch still burned, but the pain blurred into something raw, intoxicating. Every thrust wrung a ragged sound from Tanner, who wasn't quiet anymore —who was muttering filth into her skin, his hands guiding her movements.

"Yeah, just like that. Fuck. You feel—fuck—so good." His voice was wrecked. His hands slid up her ribs, thumbs brushing the underside of her breasts, pinching her nipples hard.

Blair clenched around him, her breath hitching as she adjusted to the stretch. Too much. Too fucking much. And shit, she hadn't even bottomed out yet. There was still more. How the hell was there still more of him? Tanner's grip was iron, his patience unending as he watched her face, his own jaw locked tight with restraint.

"Breathe," he growled.

She sucked in air. The stretch burned, but she wanted this. Wanted him.

"That's it," he gritted out. "Fucking—slow, Blair. Don't rush. You'll —fuck—you'll tear."

She didn't care. She wanted the ache, the heat, the way he filled her completely, the way his cock dragged against spots inside her that had never been touched before. Her ex had never stretched her like this. Never made her feel so full.

Tanner swore again, his thumbs pressing bruises into her hips as she rolled her body against his. "You're killing me," he muttered.

She dropped forward, bracing her hands on his chest, and his breath hitched. The new angle made him slide deeper, harder. A punched-out sound escaped her.

"Good?" Tanner's voice was rough, his fingers flexing against her skin.

"Uh-huh," she managed, voice wavering.

He smirked, but his eyes were pure hunger. "Bullshit." He sat up in one sharp motion, grabbing the back of her neck and pulling her into a brutal kiss. His hips rolled up into hers, and she whimpered into his mouth.

"Told you to go slow," he muttered against her lips, but he wasn't stopping her, wasn't pulling away. His free hand slid between them, thumb circling her clit. "You take me so fucking well," he breathed.

Blair shuddered. The praise pushed her higher. The pain had melted into something thick and hot, pleasure sparking under her skin with every grind of his cock inside her. She was losing rhythm, her movements uneven as sensation overwhelmed her.

Tanner took over, his grip unrelenting as he guided her, lifting her up and pulling her back down, controlling the pace. "That's it," he rasped. "Fuck, look at you. Taking all of me." He was lying. She knew there was still more, but that would have to be for another day because fuck. She wasn't going to be able to walk tomorrow.

She moaned, head dropping against his shoulder, nails biting into the hard planes of his back.

"Gonna come?" His fingers worked her clit faster, his breath hot against her ear.

She nodded, too far gone to speak.

"Good." He bit her shoulder hard. "I want to feel you come on my dick."

The words tipped her over. Pleasure ripped through her, her body tightening around him. Tanner swore as he lost control, thrusting up into her with rough, erratic movements. His breath hitched once, twice, and then he buried himself deep with a muttered curse, his release hot inside her.

"Oh. My. God." Blair whispered against his skin.

For a long moment, they just breathed.

Then Tanner leaned back, studying her face with what was the first full grin she'd seen on his mouth. "Still alive?"

Blair laughed, breathless. "Barely."

Holy shit. He had a dimple. "Good."

But his hand was gentle when he brushed her hair back from her face. "If your pussy would kindly let go of my dick, I'll go get you a washcloth."

———

BLAIR STARED AT THE SAME LINE OF CODE FOR THE FOURTH time, her brain refusing to process the neural pathway mapping data that should have been fascinating. Instead, all she could focus on was the sound of Tanner's fingers tapping against his tablet six feet away; a steady rhythm that matched the pulse between her thighs every time she remembered how those same fingers had felt inside her two nights ago.

God, she was pathetic.

She shifted in her chair, hyperaware of the dull ache in muscles she'd forgotten she had. Her body was like a fucking neon sign advertising what they'd done, every twinge a reminder of how he'd stretched her, filled her, made orgasm again and again and again and again. And now here they were, back in the sterile safety of the lab, pretending like she hadn't discovered that her fake husband had the kind of dick that rewrote her understanding of human anatomy.

"The cortisol patterns are inconsistent," she mumbled, mostly to break the silence that was making her want to climb out of her skin. The stress responses spike here, but then plateau instead of following the expected decay curve. It's like the subjects' fight-or-flight mechanisms are stuck in a feedback loop."

Kind of like her libido, actually. Stuck in a perpetual state of fight-or-flight, except instead of running, all she wanted to do was fight her way out of her clothes and onto Tanner's lap.

Tanner said nothing. Didn't even look up from whatever classified bullshit he was reading.

Blair gritted her teeth. Two days of this. Two days of him being professionally courteous and carefully distant, like he hadn't whispered filthy praise in her ear while she came apart in his hands. Like he hadn't looked at her afterward with something so raw and unguarded it had made her chest ache.

And that damn dimple hadn't made a single reappearance.

"Of course, trauma responses are notoriously difficult to predict," she continued, her voice getting that manic edge it took on when she was nervous. "The amygdala doesn't follow neat mathematical models when it comes to processing threats. It's more like a smoke detector that's been set off too many times. Eventually, it starts screaming at the smell of burnt toast instead of actual fire."

This time Tanner did look up, his dark eyes meeting hers for exactly 2.3 seconds before flicking back to his screen. But she caught it—the slight tightening around his eyes, the way his jaw flexed like he was biting back words.

Good. At least she wasn't the only one struggling with this weird limbo they'd created.

"Hungry?" he asked, standing abruptly. "I'll grab lunch."

Before she could answer, he was already moving toward the door. Blair watched him go, her gaze definitely lingering on the way his pants hugged his ass.

She was losing her fucking mind.

The moment the door closed behind him, she slumped forward and banged her forehead against her desk. The solid thunk was oddly satisfying, so she did it again.

"Get it together, Blair," she muttered to her keyboard. "You're a doctor and a scientist, not a horny teenager. You can analyze this logically."

Except logic seemed to have packed its bags and left town the moment Tanner had put his mouth between her legs. Now her brain kept shorting out every time he came within ten feet of her, flooding her system with a cocktail of dopamine and oxytocin that made higher reasoning about as effective as a chocolate teapot.

She was contemplating a third therapeutic head-bang when the door opened again. Too soon for food. Way too soon.

Blair jerked upright and rubbed her forehead, trying to look like a professional scientist instead of a woman having a sexual crisis, but froze when she saw Tanner's expression. Gone was the careful mask he'd been wearing for two days. Instead, his face was storm clouds and sharp edges, his eyes locked on hers with an intensity that made her pulse spike.

"Forgot my keys," he said, but he didn't move toward the hook where they hung by the door.

They stared at each other across the lab.

"Tanner," she started, not sure what she was going to say but knowing she had to say something before this tension killed her.

He took a step closer. Then another. Blair's breath caught as he approached her workstation. When he reached her chair, he braced one hand on her desk and the other on the back of her seat, caging her in.

"You're driving me crazy," he said, his voice low.

Blair's heart hammered against her ribs. "Good. Because you're driving me insane. Do you have any idea how hard it is to concentrate when you're sitting over there looking like—" She gestured vaguely at all of him. "Like that. And I keep thinking about the other night, about how you felt inside me, and my brain just stops working because apparently four orgasms weren't enough to get you out of my system, which is fascinating from a scientific perspective but also deeply inconvenient when I'm trying to analyze neuropathway patterns."

Tanner's pupils dilated. His gaze dropped to her mouth, and for one heart-stopping moment she thought he was going to kiss her.

Instead, his phone rang.

The sound cut through the charged air. Tanner straightened, stepping back so fast Blair felt the loss of his body heat.

"Whitney," he answered, his voice already shifting back into professional mode. Blair wanted to scream.

She watched his face change as he listened, saw the moment he clicked back into whatever dangerous world he inhabited when he wasn't playing house with her.

"When?" His free hand ran through his hair. "No, I understand. Be there in thirty."

He hung up, avoiding her eyes. "I have to go."

"What kind of go?" Blair asked, hating how small her voice sounded.

"Carson called a private meeting with the other guys. There's been a development with your case."

Her case. Right. Because that's what she was to him—a case. A job. A responsibility he'd somehow ended up fucking, which probably violated seventeen different professional codes.

"When will you be back?"

Tanner finally looked at her, and something flickered across his face before he locked it down. "I don't know." He grabbed his keys and jacket. At the door, he paused."Blair." The way he said her name made her stomach flip. "Stay here. Please." The "please" sounded strange coming from him. "I'll lock up and come back, and if not, I'll send Briggs to collect you and take you to Charlie."

"Okay," was all she could manage to say.

And then he was gone, leaving her alone with the lingering scent of his cologne and a throbbing forehead.

Blair slumped back in her chair, staring at the door he'd disappeared through.

"Fuck," she said to the empty lab. When her phone buzzed with a text from an unknown number, one that was signed by the monster who haunted her nightmares, Blair swore again. "Double fuck."

CHAPTER EIGHT

TANNER

TANNER'S DICK WAS STILL HARD FROM ALMOST KISSING HIS wife. Sitting in Crest Strategies' pristine conference room, surrounded by mahogany and leather and the kind of money that bought silence, all he could think about was Blair pressed against her desk. The way she'd babbled about neural pathways while her pupils dilated. How close he'd come to saying fuck it and tasting that smart mouth of hers.

"Tanner." Carson's voice cut through his mental replay. "Did you hear me? We've got a problem."

Tanner shifted in his chair, trying to focus on Carson's grim expression instead of the memory of Blair's vanilla scent. Around the table, the others looked like they'd been drinking battery acid. Benedict's usual smirk was gone, replaced by the kind of calculation that meant someone was about to get fucked. Penn hunched over his laptop, fingers flying across the keys as if his life depended on it. James had enough legal documents spread in front of him to paper a small country.

"What kind of problem?" Tanner asked.

"The kind that wants your wife dead," Penn said without looking up.

Every muscle in Tanner's body went rigid. "Explain."

Carson slid a file across the polished table. "Nexus isn't working alone. DARPA's involved. They want Blair's research."

Tanner's hands clenched into fists. The same cocksuckers who'd taken Annabelle, tortured her for information, then thrown her away like trash when they broke her beyond repair. His sister's face flashed through his mind; hollow eyes, track marks where the IV had been, the way she'd flinched every time someone touched her.

"How involved?" His voice came out level. Controlled even.

"Deep enough to send contractors after her instead of going in themselves," Benedict said. "That Penten asshole at the event a couple nights ago? DARPA money."

Tanner's jaw clenched so hard he thought he might crack teeth. "And?"

Penn finally looked up from his screen, glasses sliding down his nose. "There's more. The man orchestrating DARPA's interest isn't some faceless government rat."

He spun his laptop around. A photograph filled the screen; brown hair, weak chin, the kind of bland features that let predators blend into crowds. He had calculating eyes with the dead stare of someone who enjoyed causing pain.

"Ryland Michaelson," James said quietly. "Blair's ex-husband."

The world went red around the edges. His name hadn't been in any of the files Tanner had read on Blair, which was probably a good thing because how was he supposed to protect her when he was out hunting the asshole who'd tried to shatter her?

That piece of shit had spent too many goddamn years beating her down, breaking her piece by fucking piece until she'd believed she deserved it. He'd put bruises on her skin and scars on her soul and made her think she was worthless.

"Son of a fucking bitch," Tanner breathed.

"Gets worse," Penn continued. "Financial records show Michaelson's been funding surveillance on Blair for months. Even before the whistleblower event. We think he's been waiting for the right moment to—"

"To what?" Tanner's voice dropped to a growl.

"To take back what he thinks belongs to him," Benedict finished. "Her research. And her."

A dark, violent feeling twisted in Tanner's gut. His hands twitched toward the Glock holstered under his jacket. He'd spent years tracking down the men who'd destroyed his sister. Years of patient hunting before he'd put bullets in their heads. But this was different. This was Blair.

His wife.

When the fuck had that stopped being just a legal convenience?

"He's not getting near her," Tanner said.

"That's the plan," Carson agreed. "But we need to be smart. Michaelson has resources, government backing—"

"I don't give a shit what he has. He touches her, he dies."

"Christ, Tanner," James muttered. "We can't just—"

"Can't what? Protect her?" Tanner's chair scraped against the floor as he leaned forward. "You want to play politics while that fucking asshole hunts my wife?"

"Your wife," Benedict repeated, one eyebrow arched. "Interesting choice of words."

"Fuck off, Ben."

Carson held up a hand. "Enough. We're all on the same side here. The question is how we handle this."

"We eliminate the threat," Tanner said simply.

"It's not that simple," James protested. "Michaelson has DARPA protection, congressional connections—"

"So did the assholes who tortured my sister." Tanner's voice went flat. "Didn't stop me from putting them in the ground."

The room went quiet. They all knew about his sister, about what DARPA had done to her. They also knew what Tanner had done afterward. He had hunted down every man involved in Annabelle's torture and made them pay.

It hadn't brought her back. But it had felt good in the moment.

"Look," Carson said carefully, "we all understand your position. And we need Blair alive and functional to protect her research. If Michaelson plays this smart, uses their history—"

"She's not a fucking idiot. She'd never go back to him."

"No one's suggesting she would," Benedict said. "But abusers are experts at manipulation. He might try to contact her, convince her to meet—"

"Over my dead body."

Penn cleared his throat. "Actually, that brings up another point. Blair doesn't know about any of this yet, does she? About Michaelson being involved?"

Tanner shook his head. "Considering I just found out, no."

"She needs to know," Carson said. "Tonight. Before Michaelson makes his move."

The thought of telling Blair that her nightmare was hunting her made Tanner's stomach clench. She'd told him how hard she'd worked to grow after her ex. How she'd been getting stronger, more confident.

This news might shatter that progress.

"There's also the matter of her research," James continued. "If they manage to get their hands on the Vx-7 data—"

"They won't." Tanner's voice was absolute.

"Tanner, be realistic," Carson said. "If DARPA decides to play things the way they did with Annabelle—"

"Then they'll learn why they gave me an honorable discharge instead of a court martial."

Another silence.

"We should also consider extraction protocols," Benedict said eventually. "Multiple safe houses, communication blackouts—"

"I'm going back," Tanner announced, pushing his chair away from the table.

"Wait," Carson said sharply. "We're not finished."

"I am." Tanner stood. "My wife is sitting alone in a lab with no idea her fucking ex is pulling government strings to get his hands on her. You want to sit here and strategize? Fine. Send me a fucking memo."

"Your orders are to—" Carson started.

"My orders are to protect Blair," Tanner cut him off. "Everything else is just noise."

He was halfway to the door when Carson's voice stopped him.

"This isn't just about the job anymore, is it?"

Tanner looked back over his shoulder. Carson's expression was knowing, almost sympathetic. The others watched with varying degrees of understanding.

"No," Tanner said simply. "It's not."

He walked out before anyone could respond.

In the elevator, Tanner's damn hands shook as he pulled out his phone. The secure line to the lab rang once. Twice.

"Hello?" Blair's voice, but something was off. Strained.

"It's me," he said. "You okay?"

A pause. Too long. "I'm fine. Just... it's been a weird afternoon."

"Weird how?"

Another pause. "I got a text. Right after you left."

Tanner's blood turned to ice. "From who?"

"I didn't answer." Her voice was small, vulnerable in a way that made him want to put his fist through the elevator wall. "It was my ex."

Fuck. Fuck fuck fuck.

"What did he say?" Tanner growled.

"Nothing much." Blair's breathing was unsteady. "He said he missed me. That we needed to talk. That he could help with my... situation."

Rage roared through Tanner's system like wildfire. That manipulative piece of shit was already working his angles, trying to worm his way back into Blair's head.

"Blair, listen to me," he said, forcing his voice to stay calm. "Don't talk to him. Don't respond to any messages. Don't—"

"I won't." Her voice was firmer now. "I deleted the text without a second thought. But Tanner... how did he find me? I changed my number, my address, everything."

Because he has the full resources of the United States government hunting you, Tanner thought. *Because your research is worth billions, and he wants to own it. And you.*

"I'm coming back," he said instead. "Right now. We need to talk."

"About Ryland?"

"About everything."

The elevator opened onto the parking garage. Tanner was already moving toward his truck, keys in hand.

"Tanner?" Blair's voice was smaller now. "I don't need to be scared, right?"

"No," he said, taking a deep breath himself. "No, because there is no fucking way he is hurting you again. Not a fucking chance."

"But what if—"

"No what-ifs." He slammed the truck door, the engine roaring to life. "I'm fifteen minutes out. Keep the doors locked; don't answer any calls except mine."

"Okay."

He hung up and floored the accelerator. There wasn't a single fucking doubt in his mind. He'd burn the world down before he'd let Ryland Michaelson touch her again.

———

THE LAB DOOR HISSED SHUT BEHIND TANNER. HIS EYES locked onto Blair immediately—perched on a stool at the central workstation, her spine rigid, fingers tapping arrhythmically against the stainless steel surface. Still there. Still safe. The tension in his shoulders uncoiled a fraction.

She turned as he approached. Her bottom lip was raw from worrying it between her teeth, eyes wide and glassy. He crossed the room in three strides.

Tanner didn't think. He just gathered her up—one arm around her back, the other cradling the back of her head—and pulled her against his chest. Her breath hitched in quiet surprise, her body stiff for half a second before she melted into him. Her face pressed against his chest, fingers clutching his shirt.

"You're crushing me," she mumbled into his ribs, but there was no real protest in it.

He loosened his grip just enough to tilt her face up, catching the way her throat worked as she swallowed hard. "What did they tell you?" she asked.

Tanner exhaled through his nose. He should've planned how to say this. Should've eased into it. Instead, he just laid it bare: "DARPA's involved. They're working with Nexus. And your ex-husband is the one pulling their strings, trying to get to your research."

Blair went absolutely still. Her pupils dilated, lips parting on a sharp inhale. He watched the realization ripple through her; eyelids fluttering, pulse jumping in her throat. Then, her features twisted. "That *motherfucker*."

Tanner had expected tears. But shit. Rage was better.

She shoved away from him, pacing the length of the lab. "He always said I wouldn't last without him. That I'd come crawling back when I realized how naïve I was. And now he's using the fucking government to steal—"

"He won't get near you." Tanner cut in.

"You don't know Ryland. He doesn't take no for an answer." Her voice was edged with something brittle, fingers knotting in her hair. "He—Christ, the audacity—"

Tanner caught her wrist mid-gesture, pulling her back in. Her chest heaved against his. "Listen to me," he said, tipping her chin up. "He wants control. He won't get it. He wants your research? We make sure he can't fucking touch it. He wants you?" His thumb brushed the hinge of her jaw. "I will kill him."

"For me?"

"For you. But also for me. I fucking hate him."

"You've never met him."

"Says a lot, doesn't it," Tanner raised an eyebrow, and despite how unnatural it felt, he smirked at her.

Blair's breath stuttered. Her gaze flicked to his mouth.

Tanner didn't know which of them moved first. Just that one second they were staring at each other, and the next, her hands were fisted in his shirt, his mouth crashing down on hers. The kiss was all desperation, Blair arching onto her toes to meet him. He lifted her clean off the ground, her legs wrapping around his waist as he carried her backward—until her hips hit the edge of the lab bench.

He tore away only to kiss down her throat, nipping at the frantic pulse there. Blair gasped, fingers scraping through his short hair.

"Lube," she panted.

Tanner huffed a laugh against her skin. "Where?"

"Drawer—left side—sample preservation requires—" He didn't let her finish, yanking the drawer open and grabbing the small bottle of silicone-based lubricant marked *Lab Use Only*.

"Of course you have lab-grade lube," Tanner muttered, popping the cap.

Blair was already shoving her skirt up around her waist, peeling off her panties with impatient fingers. "Shut up and do something with it." That confident look in her eye was one of the sexiest things Tanner had ever seen.

He coated his fingers, dragging them through her folds. Her hips jerked at the first press, already soaked, but he wasn't taking chances. Not after last time. He worked her open slowly, curling his fingers just to hear her curse.

"Fuck, Tanner—"

"I've got you." His free hand framed her jaw, keeping her eyes on his.

Tanner watched the way Blair's breath caught when his fingers pressed in. He crooked his fingers, testing, and her thighs clenched around his wrist.

"Still sore?" He asked with a raised brow, thumb circling her clit in lazy strokes even as his fingers worked deeper.

Blair exhaled a laugh that dissolved into a moan. "Ask me if I give a damn right now."

That was all the answer he needed.

He kept the pace slow even as her hips rocked against his hand, just to watch desperation flicker in her eyes. The way her fingers dug into his forearm, blunt nails leaving marks. The flush creeping up her chest, blotchy and perfect in its disarray. Lab coat half-off one shoulder, hair coming undone.

"You're gonna come just like this," he murmured, pressing in deeper. "Won't even need my cock."

"Bullshit." Her fingers fumbled with his belt, the buckle clinking. He let her wrestle with it, focused on the way she pulsed around him, the slick slide of silicone and her own wetness coating his fingers.

"You don't think I can make you come with just my fingers?" He twisted his wrist slightly, just to hear her whimper.

Blair bit her lip, eyes flicking down to where his fingers disappeared inside her. "I think you're stalling."

Smart fucking woman.

He let go of her just long enough to shed his jacket and shrug off his shoulder holster. No weapons necessary. His pistol hit the counter with a heavy thunk as Blair finally won the war with his belt, yanking it free.

"Get these off." Her voice was wrecked already.

He caught her wrists before she could go for his zipper, pinning them to the desk beside her hips. "Not yet."

Her pulse jumped under his grip. "Tanner—"

"Tell me how bad you want it."

She rolled her eyes, but her breath hitched when he pressed his palm flat against her center, the heel of his hand grinding down in slow circles.

"Fine." Blair tilted her chin up. "I want to feel you split me open on that monster cock of yours. Better?"

Jesus.

His grip tightened on her wrists before he brought them up to his mouth, pressing a kiss to the inside of each. "Close enough." He released her.

Tanner let his wife drag his zipper down, shove his pants low enough that his cock sprang free, already flushed and heavy. Her hands wrapped around him, twisting on the upstroke, and his vision whited out for a second. He had to lean forward, bracing himself against the edge of the desk and effectively caging her in.

"Fuck—"

She smirked. "Too much?"

"Not enough," he grunted, spinning her around without warning and bending her over the desk. Her back arched, skirt still rucked up around her waist. Tanner nudged her thighs wider with his knee, guiding himself through her slick folds, teasing but not pushing in. She tensed, and since he wasn't sure why, he paused. He ran his hands down the curve of her spine, memorizing the way her muscles contracted under his touch. "Relax, Blair. I'll go slow."

"You'd better not."

Laughing hoarsely, he lined himself up and pressed in. Just the tip, just enough to make her gasp. Her body resisted, still tight and deliciously soft. Whether she knew it or not, she was clenching. "Breathe."

She sucked in a shuddering breath and he pushed deeper, inch by agonizing inch, until he was halfway in. She'd taken more of him before, but now that he was in control, he kept things slow. Even if it would be the death of him.

"Christ, Blair." He bit the words off, holding still to let her adjust.

She rocked back against him, hair slipping over her shoulder. "Move."

He did.

Slow at first, shallow thrusts that made her whimper, her fingers scrambling for purchase on the smooth metal surface. Tanner gritted his teeth as he rocked into her, the drag almost unbearable. Every muscle in his body strained with restraint; the instinct to pound into her warring with the need to keep her safe. Especially here, like this, with Blair's cheek pressed to cold stainless steel, her fingers leaving smudges on the shiny surface.

"You breathing?" He dragged his palm down the elegant arch of her spine, feeling the flutter of her ribs as she sucked in air.

She arched backward into him—impatient—hips lifting. "God, just —harder."

Tanner caught her hip with one hand, halting her. "No." His breath was jagged. "Slow, Blair. I'm in charge this time."

"Then go fucking faster," Blair groaned, frustration tightening her spine, her fingers curling against the desk. "You're torturing me."

He smirked, even though she couldn't see it, and eased out nearly all the way before pressing back in. Slow. Deliberate. Watching the way her thighs trembled, the way her breath stuttered every time he pushed a bit farther, closer and closer to bottoming out. "You'll take it just like this. Just how I give it to you."

She made a noise halfway between a growl and a whimper. Fuck, he loved that sound.

Tanner leaned over her, one forearm braced beside her head, his other hand sliding around to her front, fingers finding her clit. Blair jerked as he touched her, her back bowing.

"Easy." His lips brushed the shell of her ear. "You feel that? How tight you are?"

She exhaled a shaky laugh. "Hard to miss."

His chuckle was rough against her skin. "Good." He stroked her in time with his thrusts, each one deeper than the last, stretching her inch by inch. "You're gonna come just like this, all spread out on your fancy lab desk."

Her breath wavered, but her body was already responding, her walls fluttering around him as he worked both of them to the edge.

"Don't—oh—don't stop." Her voice was wrecked.

"Wasn't planning on it." He pressed harder, circling her clit, his cock buried deep.

Blair's fingers scrambled for something to hold onto, knocking over a pen holder. It clattered, spilling across the desk. Tanner didn't care. He was too busy watching the way her skin flushed, the way her throat worked as her breathing turned ragged.

Then she clenched around him, her whole body tensing, a sharp cry tearing free as she came. Tanner hissed, the sensation almost enough to undo him instantly. His rhythm stuttered, his grip on her hip turning bruising.

"Jesus, Blair—"

She craned her neck to look back at him, her lips parted, eyes hazy. "Don't stop."

"Fuck." He exhaled hard, forcing himself to keep moving, even as every thrust sent shocks of pleasure up his spine. She was still fluttering around him, oversensitive, but she wasn't pushing him away. If anything, she tilted her hips, taking him even deeper. With one more thrust, he'd bottomed out and she gasped his name.

His vision whited out for a second. "You trying to kill me?"

Blair smirked, breathless. "Would it work?"

Tanner dragged his teeth over the back of her neck in answer, making her gasp, then finally let go—his thrusts turning rough, uncontrolled, chasing his own release. Blair moaned beneath him, her legs shaking. He reached down, hooking an arm under her thigh to pull her harder against him, the angle shifting just enough that she whimpered.

"Tanner—fuck—"

He was right there, teetering on the edge, when his phone buzzed in his discarded jacket.

Both of them froze.

Blair twisted slightly to glare at him. "You better not fucking answer that."

Tanner barked out a laugh, then shoved back into her, one hand knotting in her hair to tip her head back. "Wasn't planning on it."

He came with her name on his lips, his hips locking as he emptied into her, the world narrowing down to heat and friction and Blair, her body still tight around him. For a long moment, all he could hear was their ragged breathing, the hum of the lab's ventilation system.

Then she slumped forward, boneless, and Tanner barely caught her before she face-planted onto the desk. When he pulled out, she winced, and his heart clenched at the same time. Fuck, if he hurt her...

He turned her in his arms, only to find her grinning up at him.

"Tell me that was all of it, because I think if there's more to this dick of yours"—she trailed a hand up his cock, and he tensed—"I might actually be concerned about my organs being rearranged."

"You took it all." He pressed a kiss to her temple, a smirk on his mouth. How was it that she could make his mouth do that when no one else could?

She rolled her eyes, but then her gaze flicked past him to the scattered contents of her workspace. Vials tipped over. Reports crumpled. Her lab coat halfway off the counter.

"Oh my God." Her voice was horrified.

Tanner followed her stare. "You're worried about the mess?"

Blair gestured weakly at the chaos. "This is weeks of data. If anything got contaminated—"

"Relax." He caught her wrist before she could scramble away from the desk. "Nothing got ruined."

She shot him a disbelieving look.

Tanner shrugged. "I made sure."

Her brows furrowed. "You what?"

"Checked everything before I bent you over. You really think I'd risk contaminating your research?" His thumb stroked her pulse point. "I know what it means to you."

Blair stared at him. Then she exhaled a shaky laugh, her fingers threading through his hair. "You're terrifying."

Tanner kissed her, then pulled back. "That's the nicest thing anyone has ever said to me."

She smiled. It was the kind that made his chest tighten.

His phone buzzed again.

Blair groaned. "Whoever that is, I hate them."

Tanner grabbed his jacket, checking the screen. Carson's name flashed up at him.

> We have Penten.

His grip tightened. The moment shattered.

Blair's expression shifted as she caught the change in him. "What's wrong?"

Tanner met her eyes. "They have Penten, the guy who tried to—"

"Kidnap me, I know." Her breath caught. The air between them shifted, the warmth of seconds ago replaced by something sharper. Something lethal. Blair didn't flinch. "Good."

Tanner handed her a clean rag from a pile labeled clean, as well as her discarded panties. "Let's go break him."

CHAPTER NINE

BLAIR

BLAIR'S HANDS WERE SHAKING, BUT NOT FROM FEAR. Standing in the doorway of the abandoned warehouse, watching Dominic Penten zip-tied to a rusted metal chair under flickering fluorescents, something dark and hungry uncurled in her chest. The man who'd tried to kidnap her looked smaller than she remembered. His left eye was already swollen shut, courtesy of Tanner's greeting when they'd dragged him here.

"Christ, Blair." Tanner's voice was low behind her. "You don't need to see this."

She turned to look at him, taking in the careful tension in his shoulders, the way his hands flexed like he was already imagining violence. This wasn't the man who'd made her see stars in the lab not two hours ago. This was someone colder, more dangerous. Someone who knew exactly how to break things. He reminded her more of the man she'd married. Closed off. Focused.

"I want to see it," she said, surprised by how steady her voice sounded. "I need to."

"Blair—"

"He tried to kidnap me. He was going to drag me back to—" She couldn't say Ryland's name. Not yet. "I'm not waiting in the car like some helpless victim."

Tanner studied her face, his dark eyes unreadable. "This won't be clean. Or quick."

"I know." Blair's hands were still shaking. She curled them into fists to hide it. "I know what you're going to do. And I know why you have to do it."

He nodded once and moved past her into the warehouse proper, rolling up his sleeves, and damn if the sight didn't send heat pooling low in her belly. That sexy, tatted, terrifying man was her husband.

Blair followed. Industrial equipment loomed in the shadows— cranes, conveyor belts, machines whose purpose she couldn't identify. But at the center of it all, pinned in that harsh circle of light, was Penten.

His good eye tracked their movement. "This is a waste of time," he said, his voice hoarse.

"My friends caught you sneaking into our building after hours," Tanner said, his tone conversational. "I'd like to know why."

"Go to hell."

"Been there. Got the T-shirt. Now tell me what you were doing in Crest Strategies."

"I'm just a contractor. I don't know anything useful."

"We'll see about that." Tanner's voice remained almost friendly. The false pleasantness made Blair's skin prickle.

Tanner moved to the tool table someone had thoughtfully provided, selecting a wrench with the same care Blair might use choosing a scalpel. Her scientific brain immediately began cataloging potential applications—blunt force trauma, leverage for joint manipulation, pressure point stimulation.

"Let's start simple," Tanner said, testing the weight of the wrench. "Who hired you to grab my wife?"

My wife. The possessiveness in those words sent another spike of heat through Blair's system.

"I told you, I don't—"

The wrench connected with Penten's kneecap with a wet crack that reverberated through the warehouse. His scream bounced off concrete walls and steel beams.

Blair didn't flinch. Didn't look away. Instead, she stepped closer, her pulse hammering with something that definitely wasn't fear.

"Interesting choice," she heard herself say. "The patella is mostly cartilage and ligaments. Incredibly painful to damage, but not immediately life-threatening."

Both men stared at her. Penten with horror, Tanner with something like admiration in his eye.

"Of course," Blair continued, her voice taking on that lecture-hall tone she used when explaining complex concepts, "if you really wanted to maximize pain without permanent damage, you'd target the nerve clusters instead. The ulnar nerve, for instance. Or the peroneal nerve just below the fibular head."

"Is that so?" Tanner's voice was carefully neutral, but she caught the slight rasp, the way his grip tightened on the wrench.

"Mm." Blair moved closer to Penten, studying him. "Nerve pain is disproportionate to actual tissue damage. It's one of the many reasons I started studying it. You know, a relatively small injury to the right spot can cause agony that feels completely out of scale with the actual trauma inflicted."

Her hands had stopped shaking. That surprised her. She felt calm now, focused, like she was back in her lab analyzing data. Except the data was human suffering, and she was finding it far more engaging than she should.

"You're fucking insane," Penten whimpered, staring at her like she'd grown fangs.

"Maybe," Blair said mildly. "But I'm also a neuroscientist. And I spent too many fucking years married to a man who was very, very creative when it came to inflicting pain without leaving visible marks. You learn things."

Tanner's eyes sharpened. "Careful."

She looked at him, caught the warning, the concern. He was likely worried about her. Worried that this was too much, too dark, too far from the woman he thought he knew.

If only he knew how far she'd already fallen after living with Ryland.

"May I?" she asked, nodding toward the wrench.

For a moment, Tanner didn't move. He searched her face, looking for—what? Hesitation? Regret? Whatever he was looking for, he didn't find it. Instead, he held out the tool, his fingers brushing hers as she took it.

The metal was warm from his grip. Heavier than she'd expected. She tested its weight, found the balance point, considered leverage and impact angles with the same analytical consideration she'd apply to any experiment.

"The ulnar nerve runs right along here," she said, positioning herself beside Penten's chair, tracing the path with her free hand. "It's what causes that shooting pain when you hit your funny bone. Except this won't be funny at all."

She placed the wrench against the spot she'd indicated, applying just enough pressure to make her point. Penten went rigid, a strangled sound escaping his throat.

"Now," Blair said conversationally, "why don't you tell us what you wanted at Crest Strategies? Because I have a very detailed understanding of human anatomy, and honestly? I'm curious to see how accurate my theoretical knowledge is when applied practically."

"Jesus Christ," Penten gasped. "You're both psychotic."

Blair increased the pressure slightly, watching as Penten's back arched, tendons standing out in his neck. The control was intoxicating. After years of being powerless, of being hurt and broken and discarded, she finally held the power to inflict instead of endure.

It felt better than she'd expected.

"DARPA," Penten finally choked out. "It's DARPA. They wanted you and your research." He cried out when she pressed harder, the words tumbling out as if he couldn't speak them fast enough. "They sent me to find out where you were. Please, for the love of god, stop!"

Blair eased off the pressure but kept the wrench in position. "Specifically who at DARPA?"

"Michaelson. Ryland Michaelson. He's been hunting you for months."

Her vision grayed at the edges, her composure cracking. Ryland. She'd known it was Ryland. But hearing it confirmed... She struggled to swallow.

"Blair." Tanner's voice grounded her, and she took a shaky breath. When she met his gaze, she nodded once.

"What does he want with my research?"

"The Vx-7 compound. He thinks it can be weaponized."

"Weaponized how?" Tanner moved closer, close enough that Blair could feel his body heat, smell his cologne.

Penten's good eye darted between them, calculating. "Neural control. Mind control. The compound can affect brain chemistry, right? Michaelson thinks if they modify it right, they can use it to make people compliant. Soldiers who can't disobey orders. Civilians who won't question government policy. A whole population of puppets."

The world tilted sideways. Blair's legs went weak, the wrench suddenly too heavy in her hand. It clattered to the floor. Her research —her life's work, designed to help people with spinal injuries regain neural function—perverted into a tool of oppression. The Vx-7 was supposed to heal, to restore, to give people back their lives.

Not steal their free will.

What the actual hell? When had she walked into some shitty dystopian novel?

"That's not—" Her voice cracked. "That's not how it works. The compound doesn't control thoughts; it facilitates neural pathway reconstruction—"

"Doesn't matter what it's supposed to do," Penten interrupted. "Michaelson's convinced it can be adapted. He's got a whole team at Nexus working on modifications. Says with the right delivery system, the right dosage, they can turn your healing serum into liquid compliance."

Bile rose in Blair's throat. All those late nights in the lab, all those careful calculations, all that hope for helping paralyzed patients walk again—and Ryland wanted to turn it into a weapon. Into chains for the human mind. The man got hard from controlling others.

"Where?" Tanner's voice was deadly quiet.

"I don't know. Above my pay grade."

Blair picked up the wrench from the ground and pressed it against the nerve cluster again, harder this time. Penten's scream was sharper, more desperate. She felt Tanner's eyes on her, felt his surprise at her ruthlessness. Part of her should have been ashamed. Instead, she felt powerful. Maybe she was just as twisted as her ex.

"Think harder," she said.

"I don't—fuck—I really don't know! Michaelson keeps everything compartmentalized. I just grab people; I don't get briefings on research facilities!"

"But you know something," Tanner said, moving to Blair's other side. They flanked Penten now.

The positioning put Tanner close enough that Blair could feel his breathing, could sense the controlled violence humming under his skin. When his arm brushed hers, she shivered.

"Who else is involved?" Tanner asked, stepping closer.

"I don't know names, I don't know specifics. I just—"

The lights cut out.

Complete, absolute darkness swallowed the warehouse. Blair heard Tanner curse, heard the scrape of his boots as he moved toward her. But before he could reach her, before she could process what was happening, the sound of footsteps echoed from the darkness— multiple sets, moving together. Too many. Too organized.

Penten's voice cut through the black. "Too late," he said, the smile evident in his voice. "He already has almost everything he needs. And now he knows exactly where to find his missing wife. He's right on time."

CHAPTER TEN

TANNER

The darkness was absolute. Tanner's hand shot out instinctively, finding Blair's shoulder in the black. Every nerve in his body screamed threat, military training kicking in as his other hand went to the Glock holstered under his jacket. The footsteps were getting closer—at least six men.

He'd expected this. He remembered what had happened with his sister. DARPA didn't fuck around when they wanted something, and they'd want Blair's research badly enough to send their best. Professional soldiers, not the contractors they'd dealt with before.

"Stay behind me," he breathed in Blair's ear, pulling her against his back.

"Tanner—"

"Quiet."

He counted heartbeats, tracked movement by sound. These weren't amateurs. The way they moved, the discipline of their approach—these were the kind of operators who could ghost through a building and leave no witnesses. The fact that they were both still breathing meant they had orders to take Blair alive. And by the sound of gun safeties going off, they were likely also directed to eliminate anyone who got in their way.

A red dot appeared in the darkness, sweeping left to right. Yeah. Shit. Laser sight. Then another. Three more. But none of them were tracking toward Blair's position. They needed her breathing.

Him? Not so much.

"Dr. Winters," a voice called. Tanner ground his teeth, but refrained from correcting it to her actual last name. His last name. It wasn't worth giving away their location. "We know you're here. This doesn't have to get messy. Just come with us, and nobody gets hurt."

Tanner almost snorted. Like hell nobody would get hurt. These bastards weren't here for a friendly chat.

He grabbed Blair's hand, pulling her toward the maze of industrial equipment to their right. If they could reach the conveyor belt system, maybe find cover that would give him angles—

"Taser, taser, taser!" The shout came from somewhere on their left.

Electrodes sparked off the concrete beside them, trailing wire. Non-lethal takedown attempts for Blair. But the muzzle flash that erupted from Tanner's right was definitely trying to put holes in him.

The sharp crack of gunfire echoed through the warehouse as bullets sparked off concrete and steel around them. Tanner shoved Blair behind a massive piece of machinery, his body shielding hers as more shots rang out. His shoulder pressed against hers, and even in the middle of a goddamn firefight, part of his brain registered how right it felt to have her there, to be protecting her.

"Can you see anything?" Blair whispered. Christ, his wife had nerves of steel.

"Enough." Tanner drew his weapon, checking the magazine by feel. Fifteen rounds. Had to make them count. "When I start shooting, you run for that office." He pointed toward a glass-walled structure barely visible in the shadows. "Lock yourself in and don't come out until I come for you."

"What if you don't—"

"I will." He turned to look at her, even though he could barely make out her face in the darkness. But he could feel her gaze searching for him, could sense her fear and her trust in equal measure. "I promise. I'll come for you."

Another burst of gunfire. Closer this time. They were being herded, pushed toward the center of the warehouse where there'd be no cover. Time to move.

Tanner counted to three, then rolled out from behind their shelter, firing twice at the nearest muzzle flash. Someone screamed. One down.

"Go!" he shouted to Blair.

He laid down covering fire as she ran, emptying half his magazine to keep the shooters pinned down. In the strobing light of muzzle flashes, he caught glimpses of tactical gear, night vision goggles, military-grade weapons. Standard kit for a black ops extraction. They'd come prepared for resistance.

Too bad for them, he wasn't planning to make this easy.

Blair reached the office, the door slamming shut behind her with a sound that made his chest tight with relief. Good. Now he could focus on staying alive long enough to get them both out of here.

A figure appeared to his left, night vision giving him away in the ambient light. Tanner put two in his chest, watching him drop like a sack of cement. Two down. But more were moving to flank him, using the machinery for cover just like he was.

BANG.

His shoulder exploded in fire. The impact spun him sideways, fresh blood immediately soaking through his shirt. They'd actually managed to hit him, but after testing the arm, it still worked. Mostly. The bullet had gone clean through, missing bone but tearing through muscle and tissue in a way that made his whole left side scream. It was almost as bad as the IED. Almost.

Three more shots came from his right. Tanner ducked, returning fire, but his clip was running low and his aim was getting sloppy as blood loss started to affect his vision. He had one spare magazine. After that, things would get very interesting very quickly.

Movement behind him. Tanner spun, firing blind, hearing a grunt as his shot found home. Three down. But his wounded shoulder screamed in protest with every move.

"Whitney!" Penten's voice called from the darkness, and Tanner

132

swore under his breath. He should've killed the asshole when he'd had the chance. "This can end easy. Just give us the bitch and walk away. You've got no stake in this."

Like hell he didn't. The woman was his wife. She was his to protect. *His.*

Tanner changed position, using a crane housing for cover. His shoulder was on fire, each heartbeat sending fresh waves of agony through the wound. Blood loss was making him lightheaded, but he could still fight. Still protect Blair.

His wife. When the fuck had that stopped being just about the mission? When had that brilliant woman become more important to him than the contract that had brought them together?

Another shooter tried to advance on his position. Tanner waited until he was close, then put a bullet in his head. The man dropped like a puppet with cut strings. Four down. How many more were out there?

The answer came as fresh gunfire from three different directions. They were coordinating now, boxing him in, and his ammunition was almost gone.

Tanner made a decision that went against every tactical instinct he'd ever been taught. He sprinted toward a cluster of storage containers, diving behind them just as bullets chewed up the ground where he'd been standing. The move cost him—his shoulder screamed, but he'd bought himself time.

And found something potentially useful. A maintenance door, partially hidden behind the containers. It led to a network of storage closets and utility rooms that might give him options. Maybe even a way to circle back to Blair without walking through the kill zone they'd set up.

He slipped inside, grateful for the solid walls between him and the shooters. His breathing was harsh in the confined space, shoulder throbbing with each heartbeat as if someone were driving nails into the wound. He needed to regroup, reassess. Figure out how to get Blair out of this alive.

The door of the office where he'd left her was maybe fifty yards away. Might as well have been fifty miles with hostiles between them, but he had to try. Had to get to her before they found another way in.

Tanner crept through the utility corridors, following them toward the office complex.

He was almost there when he heard it. Glass breaking. Shouts. Then Blair's voice.

"Get your fucking hands off me!"

That was his woman. Still fighting even when they had her cornered.

Tanner's blood turned to ice, but not from fear. From pure, undiluted rage. They had their hands on his wife.

He burst from the utility corridor, firing at the two men who were trying to restrain Blair. One dropped immediately, Tanner's shot taking him center mass. The other was using Blair as a human shield, backing toward the warehouse entrance, but being careful not to hurt her. They needed her intact.

"Let her go," Tanner snarled, his weapon trained on the man's head. He had a clean shot, but not without risking Blair.

"I don't think so." The shooter's voice was calm. "Boss wants to see his wife."

Blair's eyes found Tanner's across the distance. Even in the dim light, he could see her terror. But also her determination. She wasn't giving up. Wasn't breaking. Christ, he loved that about her.

Loved. He loved Blair. Loved his wife. Not just the sex, not just the partnership, but everything about her. Her beautiful mind, her stubborn courage, the way she looked at him like he was worth something instead of just a weapon to be pointed at problems.

And he might lose her before he ever got the chance to tell her.

The shooter made a mistake. He loosened his grip on Blair for just a moment to adjust his hold. Blair drove her elbow into his ribs, breaking free and running toward Tanner as more boots pounded up from behind. She was magnificent.

"Storage closet," Tanner pointed to a door ten feet away. "Now."

They reached it together, Tanner slamming the door and throwing the deadbolt just as the pounding started on the other side. The space was tiny, barely big enough for both of them, filled with cleaning supplies and maintenance equipment. But it was solid, defensible. For now.

"Are you hurt?" Blair's hands were on him immediately, finding the blood on his shoulder. "Oh fuck, Tanner, you're bleeding everywhere."

"It's nothing." He tried to pull away, but she held fast, her fingers probing the wound until he hissed under his breath.

"Bullshit. This is a through-and-through, but it looks like it might've nicked the subclavian artery. You're losing too much blood, and if you don't get medical attention soon—"

She was right. He could feel it—the weakness creeping in, his vision blurring at the edges from blood loss. But they didn't have time for medical attention. They had maybe minutes before the bastards outside found a way in.

"There." He pointed up at a ventilation grate near the ceiling. "Can you fit through that?"

Blair followed his gaze, understanding immediately dawning in her eyes. "What about you?"

"I'll be right behind you."

Another lie. With his shoulder fucked and blood pouring out of him, he'd never make it through the vent system. Not to mention he'd be too large. But Blair could fit. Blair could get out, get to safety, get to Carson and tell him everything they'd learned.

"Tanner—"

He silenced her with a kiss. Soft at first, almost tentative, then desperate as she melted against him and he realized this might be the last chance he ever got to taste her. When they broke apart, her eyes were bright and moist. God, she looked terrified.

"Listen to me," he said, gripping her face with his good hand, memorizing every detail of her features. "You have to get out of here. Get to Carson and the others, tell him everything Penten said. Tell him about Michaelson, about what they want to do with your research."

"I'm not leaving you." Her voice was fierce, even if it did tremble. God, he loved that about her too.

"Yes, you are." His voice was harder now. The tone that had made men follow him into impossible situations. "Because I'm not the one they want. You are. If Michaelson gets his fucking hands on you, if he gets your research, we're looking at a worldwide security threat. Millions of people could die—mind-controlled soldiers, compliant populations, entire countries turned into puppets."

"Stop." Her voice broke, tears spilling down her cheeks. "Don't do this."

"I have to." He kissed her again, harder this time, pouring everything he couldn't say into the desperate contact. All the words he should have said weeks ago, all the feelings he'd been too much of a coward to acknowledge. "You're the only one who can stop him, Blair. But only if you survive and stay out of his grasp."

The pounding on the door was getting more violent, more systematic. Soon they'd break through. Time was running out.

"You're going." He didn't let her argue. Reaching into his pocket, he pulled out the keys to the SUV they'd driven there and pressed them into her hand. She gaped at the keys in her hand for a second before a sob escaped her lips. He clenched his jaw and tried to ignore how the sound had twisted his insides. Instead, Tanner boosted Blair toward the vent, ignoring the agony that shot through his shoulder with the movement. She climbed reluctantly, looking back at him through the grate with an expression that broke something inside his chest.

"Tanner—"

"Go." He grunted.

She stared at him for a moment longer, her eyes searching his face like she were trying to memorize it. Then she nodded once and disappeared into the ductwork.

As soon as she was gone, Tanner collapsed against the wall. He brought his hand up to his shoulder and swore. But worse than the bullet hole in his shoulder was the pain sprouting in his heart. He should have told her. Should have said the words that had been building in his chest for weeks, maybe longer.

He was in love with her. Completely in love with his wife.

The door exploded inward in a shower of splinters and twisted metal. Tanner drew his gun, his remaining ammunition making every shot count. He took down two more before his magazine ran dry, then it was hand-to-hand combat in the cramped space, using every dirty trick he'd learned in two tours and a dozen black ops missions.

But blood loss won out. His movements got sluggish, his vision tunneling as his body started shutting down non-essential functions. When the fourth man finally got behind him, Tanner felt the knife slide between his ribs like liquid fire.

He went down hard, blood pooling beneath him on the concrete floor. His breathing was ragged, each inhale sending fresh waves of agony through his chest. The metallic taste of blood filled his mouth.

Boots approached. Military issue, polished to a shine despite the warehouse dust and violence.

A figure crouched beside him, and Tanner stared up into a face he recognized from the meeting with his friends. The man of Blair's nightmares. Ryland Michaelson tilted his head as he grinned down at Tanner with sharp, bright white teeth. It looked like something out of the horror movies he used to watch with Annabelle growing up.

"Tanner Whitney," Michaelson said, his voice cultured, almost pleasant. Like they were meeting at a cocktail party instead of a warehouse full of corpses. "My wife's new plaything. It's nice to finally meet you."

"Fuck you," Tanner wheezed, blood speckling his lips.

Michaelson smile widened. "Where is she, Whitney? Where's my wife?"

"She's not your f-fucking wife. Go to hell."

"Technically, she is. The divorce never finalized. She ran, you know. Changed her name, got a new ID. A new job. Hell, she moved all the way across the country. Her name used to be Rebecca. Becky Michaelson." His voice turned conversational, almost friendly in a way that made Tanner's skin crawl. "I spent years molding her, shaping her into something useful. Teaching her what happens when she disobeys. And then you come along, thinking you can just take what belongs to me?"

Tanner tried to lunge at him, but his body wouldn't cooperate.

More blood leaked onto the concrete, forming a dark pool beneath his chest.

"The thing about Becky," Michaelson continued, reaching out to adjust Tanner's position like he was arranging furniture, "is that she responds so well to the right kind of motivation. A little pain, a little fear, a little fuck, and she becomes wonderfully compliant. I'm looking forward to reminding her of that. Of teaching her what happens to people who think they can run away from me."

Rage gave Tanner enough strength to force words through his damaged throat. "Touch her and I'll fucking kill you, you son of a bitch."

Michaelson laughed, the sound echoing off the warehouse walls like breaking glass. "With what? You're bleeding out on my floor, soldier boy. In about ten minutes, you'll be nothing but a memory."

He stood, brushing dust from his knees. "Don't worry, though. I'll take very good care of Becky, or should I say, Blair. She and I have so much catching up to do. Starting with a long, detailed discussion about what happens to people who run away from me. About consequences. About pain."

The casual cruelty in his voice made Tanner's vision red at the edges. Or maybe that was the blood loss. This was the bastard who'd spent years breaking Blair down, convincing her she was worthless, that she deserved the abuse. The man who'd put scars on her soul that might never heal. The reason she flinched when someone moved too quickly next to her. The reason she hunched her shoulders when doubt crept in. The reason she'd been fine with hurting herself during sex.

This bastard had tried to shatter her.

Shatter Tanner's cunning, funny, bright, gorgeous wife.

"You're fucking dead, Michaelson," Tanner spat out, grunting as he struggled to keep his focus straight.

"Sure, buddy." Michaelson nodded to one of his men, who produced a syringe filled with something that glowed faintly blue in the warehouse lighting. "But first, we're going to have some fun with you. See how well my modified Vx-7 works on unwilling subjects. It's not perfect since I'm missing Becky's research, but it's pretty close to a finished product. Consider yourself a beta tester for the new world order."

The needle bit into Tanner's neck. Whatever they injected burned like acid through his veins, setting every nerve ending on fire. His thoughts became sluggish and strange, though that could've been from the injuries.

"Don't worry," Michaelson said, drawing back his foot and driving it into Tanner's ribs with enough force to crack bone. Tanner cried out. The pain was immediate and nauseating, but somehow distant, like it was happening to someone else. "You won't die. That would be wasteful. But by the time I'm done with you, you'll wish you had."

Another kick, this one to his wounded shoulder. Tanner's vision went white with agony, but he couldn't seem to make his body respond properly. Even his scream came out as nothing but a moan. The drug was doing something to his nervous system, scrambling the signals between his brain and his muscles.

"You see," Michaelson continued, crouching down again so his face was inches from Tanner's, "I have plans for my wife's research. Big plans. I need test subjects. And congratulations! You just volunteered to help me perfect the process."

Tanner's vision dimmed at the edges, his consciousness slipping away as the drug took hold. But he managed to force out one last message through bloody teeth, putting every ounce of hatred and defiance he could muster into the words: "Fuck yourself, you sick piece of shit."

Even as consciousness faded, Tanner held onto one thought that burned brighter than the pain, stronger than the fear: Blair was free. The asshole didn't have her. Blair was alive. She'd gotten away.

And she'd better stay that way. Because when he got out of this—and he would get out of this, no matter what it took—he had something very important to tell her.

He was in love with his wife.

"You really need to work on your vocabulary, soldier boy." Michaelson's boot connected with his skull, and darkness finally claimed him.

CHAPTER ELEVEN

BLAIR

"—AND THEN THE LIGHTS WENT OUT AND THERE WERE footsteps everywhere. Tanner told me to run and I heard him fighting. I don't know if he's—"

"Blair." Benedict's calm voice cut through her rambling. "Breathe."

She was sitting in Crest Strategies' main conference room, wrapped in Benedict's suit jacket because her own clothes were torn and filthy from crawling through ventilation ducts for what felt like hours. The words kept tumbling out of her mouth in an endless stream of panic and guilt.

"I left him," she whispered. "He boosted me into that vent and I left him there to die and I don't even know if he's still—"

"Stop." Carson's voice was sharp. He stood at the head of the table, his usually immaculate appearance disheveled, his steel-gray eyes blazing. "Tanner made his choice. He got you out. Now we get him back."

"How?" James demanded, legal documents scattered across the mahogany table like he'd been throwing them around. His perfect composure from the first few times she'd met him had cracked, worry lines etched deep around his eyes. "We don't know where they took him. We don't know if he's even—"

"He's alive." Carson growled. "They wouldn't have taken a corpse, and our people didn't find him among the people he killed."

Penn looked up from his laptop, his eyes red-rimmed behind his glasses. "I've been tracking every vehicle that left the warehouse area. Three black SUVs, all heading in different directions. Traffic cams lost them after—" His voice cracked. "Fuck. I should have had better surveillance on that location. I should have seen this coming."

"This isn't your fault," Benedict said quietly, though his usual unflappable demeanor had cracks showing around the edges too. "None of us saw this coming."

"The hell we didn't." Carson slammed his hand against the table. "DARPA's been hunting Blair's research for months. We knew Michaelson was involved. We should have been prepared for—"

"For what?" Jenna interrupted from her position by the windows, her auburn hair pulled back in a severe braid, her green eyes scanning the street below. "For a full military extraction team? Mr. Crest, from what I saw, they came with enough firepower to level a city block. This wasn't some contractor grab-and-go. This was war."

Blair pulled the jacket tighter around her shoulders, trying to stop the trembling that had started the moment she'd left Tanner behind in the vents. "You don't understand. It wasn't random. Ryland—he knew exactly where we'd be. He planned this. And if he took Tanner alive..."

She stopped, her brain catching up to her mouth. She didn't actually know why Ryland had taken Tanner instead of killing him. She'd heard Tanner fighting, heard him go down, then silence. For all she knew, he was already dead.

"Then what?" Benedict asked gently.

"I don't know." The admission felt like swallowing glass. "I just know that when I was crawling through those vents, I could hear voices. Ryland was talking to someone, giving orders about transport and containment. He said something about Vx-7, but I couldn't hear everything and I was trying to get to the exit."

The words were coming out in a rush again as she tried to process trauma through data and analysis. Meanwhile, her heart screamed that she'd abandoned the most important person in her world.

"Blair." Benedict moved his chair closer to hers. "Look at me."

She met his ice-blue eyes.

"Tanner knew the risks when he told you to run. He made that choice because keeping you safe was more important to him than anything else. Don't make his sacrifice meaningless by falling apart now."

"But what if he's—" She couldn't say the word 'dead.' Couldn't even think it without her chest tightening to the point where she couldn't breathe.

"Then we make the bastards pay," Carson said, his voice carrying a cold fury. "But first, we find out for sure."

Penn's fingers flew across his keyboard. "I'm pulling satellite footage from the warehouse area. If I can track which route they actually took—"

"How long will that take? Hours?" James asked, running his hands through his hair. "Hours we don't have. If they're planning to—" He stopped himself, glancing at Blair.

"Planning what?" she demanded.

"Nothing. We don't know anything for certain."

"Don't lie to me." Blair stood abruptly, Benedict's jacket falling off her shoulders. "You think they're going to torture him. You think they're going to kill him. You think—"

"We think Michaelson wants leverage," Benedict said calmly. "Tanner is valuable to us, which makes him valuable to Michaelson as a bargaining chip."

Blair took a step back. That was it. They were right. If Ryland had taken Tanner, it would be as leverage, but not leverage on the Crest Strategies men.

"He wants me," she whispered, and everyone looked at her. "He'll use Tanner to hurt me." Blair's fingers trembled as she paced the length of the conference room. "He'll torture him, and not just to find out where the research is. Ryland's obsessive. When I ran, he turned our entire social circle into informants. He'll use Tanner to get to me because..." Her voice cracked. "Because legally, I'm still Rebecca Michaelson."

Silence.

She watched understanding flicker across each face. Only Jenna looked confused. "What do you mean, still?"

"I tried to leave him three times before it stuck." Blair forced the words out through the tightness in her throat. "First time, he 'forgot' to file the paperwork. Second time, he threatened my mother. Third time, he dragged me back from the airport by my hair." Her fingers ghosted over her scalp out of habit. "So I waited. Planned. Brought home a paralytic from the lab. Just enough to keep him unconscious for twelve hours while I erased every trace of myself."

Penn's fingers stilled on his keyboard. "You drugged your ex-husband and disappeared?"

"After I scrubbed our shared devices, siphoned half our accounts, and drove to Nevada with cash. Yes. My mother knew people who could bury Rebecca Michaelson and exhume Blair Winters with paperwork dating back to birth. I thought it was over."

James leaned forward, arms braced on the table. "But the marriage was never dissolved."

"No. And now Ryland's fucking pissed." The walls felt like they were closing in. "He found me. He waited. All this time, he could've exposed me, but he didn't—because he's always wanted me scared and compliant first. And if he can get me back while also working his job for DARPA, he'll get everything he wants." Her pacing grew frantic. "And Tanner—" Her breath hitched. "Tanner's leverage. Ryland knows I wouldn't break for myself, but for someone else? For him?"

Benedict's voice was quiet. "You care about Tanner that much?"

She stopped dead, her pulse hammering. Yes. Yes, her mind screamed. She cared for Tanner more than she'd cared for anyone in a very, *very* long time. Clearing her throat, she nodded. "He took a bullet for me. He pushed me into a vent while he stayed behind to die." Her voice climbed. "Of course I—" She bit down hard on the rest.

Blair's phone buzzed. She glanced at it, then froze.

"What is it?" Benedict asked, and when she showed him, he paled. "Penn, can you trace this." He took the phone and turned the screen toward everyone else: a single image of Tanner, shirtless, strapped to a metal chair with medical grade restraints. His left shoulder was bandaged as well as his ribs. He was alive. Conscious. Furious. Below it, a message:

> Come home, Becky. Or the next photo won't
> be so pretty.

The room erupted into motion—Penn typing furiously, Jenna barking orders into her comms, James snatching up legal files—but Blair stood rooted to the spot, staring at the blood drying at the corner of Tanner's mouth. Ryland had him.

Oh, god, Ryland had Tanner.

"Blair, hey," Benedict put his hand on her shoulder and she flinched. "Let's go somewhere else while—"

"No. What's the plan?" Blair asked, surprised by how steady her voice sounded when everything inside her was screaming. "I want to help."

"It's better that you—"

"We find him," Carson cut Benedict off, stepping next to Blair.

"How?" Blair asked.

"However we have to." Carson's eyes were hard as steel. Glancing over his shoulder at the others in the room, Carson spoke. "Penn, I want every Nexus facility within a four-hour drive of that warehouse. I want financial records, property holdings, shell companies, everything."

"Already on it," Penn muttered. "I can't track that text, by the way. I'll keep trying though."

"Good. James, what kind of legal pressure can we bring to bear on DARPA?"

"Limited," James admitted. "If they claim national security, we're fucked. But I can make some calls, see if anyone's willing to talk off the record."

"Do it. Jenna, I want every military contact you have activated. Someone knows something about black site facilities in the area."

Jenna nodded grimly. "I'll make the calls."

"What about me?" Blair asked.

Carson looked at her for a long moment, and she saw something calculating in his expression. "You're going to help us understand exactly what Michaelson's capable of. How the hell he's planning to use your research for mind control."

"Okay, but I've already told you everything I know about the Vx-7 compound—"

"Not the science," Carson interrupted. "The man. You were married to him. You know how he thinks, how he operates. We need to get inside his head."

Blair's stomach clenched. The last thing she wanted to do was think about Ryland, about those years of psychological and physical abuse. But if it would help them find Tanner...

"He's methodical," she said slowly. "Everything has to serve a purpose. He doesn't do anything just for cruelty's sake—the cruelty is always a means to an end. Control, compliance, breaking down resistance. Ryland always saw people as experimental subjects. Guinea pigs for his theories about control and manipulation." Blair's voice was getting stronger as her analytical mind kicked in, pushing down the panic. "If he's modifying the Vx-7 compound, he'll need test subjects to see how effective his changes are."

The room went silent.

"Jesus Christ," Penn whispered. "That's inhuman."

"Well, he's the devil, so yeah," Blair muttered.

"If Michaelson needs test subjects, he needs facilities equipped for medical research. That narrows down our search parameters," Carson said.

Penn was already typing furiously. "Alright. I'm cross-referencing Nexus properties with medical equipment purchases, pharmaceutical supply chains, anything that could support human experimentation..."

"How long?" Carson asked.

"Give me two hours."

"Done."

Blair sat back down in one of the chairs, her body suddenly very tired. "I should have stayed with him," she whispered.

"Then you'd both be captured, and Michaelson would have everything he needs," Benedict said, appearing beside her. "Tanner knew that. It's why he made the choice he did."

"But what if Ryland—"

"Don't do that to yourself. The what if's. Tanner Whitney is the most stubborn, determined bastard I've ever met. He's not going to die until he's sure you're safe."

"I love him," she said, more to herself, but everyone else clearly heard her. "I don't know when that happened in this shitstorm, but it did. I love Tanner, and I can't stand the idea of Ryland hurting him," she said as she met Carson's gaze. "I'm not leaving my husband in the hands of that monster."

Carson nodded once, his gaze assessing as he looked her up and down. "Then let's get him back."

Penn looked up from his laptop, his eyes bright with the first hope she'd seen since arriving. "I've got something. Three facilities that match our parameters, all within driving distance of the warehouse."

"Which one are they at?" Carson asked.

"That's the problem. Any of them could be the right location. Or it could be none of them." Penn turned his screen around to show them a map with three red dots. "But we're going to have to check them all. Briggs?"

"I'll send three teams and report back," Jenna said, already moving towards the door. It closed behind her.

"I need my other computers to keep working on all of this." Penn swiped his laptop from the table and left too. "I'll text you when I find something." He left too, and James departed soon after.

Carson's phone rang, and he answered it with a voice gentler than Blair had heard before. "Hey. No, I'm still at work." Carson sighed and ran a hand through his hair. "No, he's still missing. I—" He glanced at Blair before covering the bottom of the phone. "I'm going to talk to Kinsley in my office. Ben, make sure Blair has what she needs." With that, he too left the conference room.

"Have you eaten?" Benedict asked Blair, drawing her attention from the door. She shook her head. "Come on. I was going to get dinner with Paisley before all of this happened. I'll introduce you."

146

CHAPTER TWELVE

BLAIR

BLAIR PRESSED HER BACK AGAINST THE COLD CONCRETE wall, her breath shallow and controlled. The facility was exactly as Jenna had described when she'd informed Carson and the others what they'd found during their first reconnaissance mission to the three Nexus buildings. Low security perimeter, minimal cameras, just enough to look nondescript. Too nondescript.

She waited until the last of the guards disappeared around the corner before peeling herself from the shadows. Her fingers trembled, not from fear, but adrenaline. Jenna had called this location "least likely," which meant they'd check it last. Tanner didn't have that kind of time.

And that's why she directly disobeyed Carson's order to go back to the safehouse at Location Charlie and wait until Jenna's people did their jobs.

She couldn't leave her husband to that monster.

Ducking behind an overflowing dumpster, Blair held her breath as the sweep of a flashlight cut across the alley. The stench of rotting garbage burned her nostrils, but she stayed still.

She counted the seconds between patrols, then darted toward the rusted service entrance. The door creaked open just wide enough for her to slip through. Darkness swallowed her. The hum of industrial air conditioning masked her footsteps as she moved deeper into the facility's underbelly. Concrete corridors branched off like veins, pipes snaking along the ceiling. She mapped the turns in her head.

A distant clang froze her mid-step. Voices echoed, too close.

"—subject still stable overnight?"

"Vitals holding. Michaelson is pleased."

Blair's pulse hammered in her throat. She edged forward, pressing herself into an alcove as two technicians passed by in white lab coats.

"You seen the scans? Neural pathways lit up like a Christmas tree. Whatever cocktail they injected him with—"

One of them jerked his head toward the hallway Blair hid in. She flattened herself against the wall, breath trapped behind clenched teeth.

The other technician laughed. "Relax. Only ghosts down here."

They moved on, boots scuffing against stained linoleum. Blair exhaled sharply and peeled away from the wall. Her fingers trembled against the cool metal of a door handle marked *Authorized Personnel Only*.

Inside, the hum of machinery filled the sterile space. Glass-walled rooms lined the corridor, each containing a single occupied exam table. Her stomach twisted at the sight of IV lines snaking into limp arms, the rhythmic beep of monitors the only sign of life. None of the figures stirred. She held her breath, only releasing it when she didn't see Tanner among them.

Maybe that was good; maybe it wasn't.

Blair's fingers curled around the edge of a metal shelving unit as she crept deeper into the facility. A shadow shifted at the end of the corridor.

She ducked behind a supply cart, pulse hammering. The squeak of rubber soles on linoleum grew louder, and two guards rounded the corner, their radios crackling with static.

Breathe. Stay still.

One of them paused, scanning the hallway. Blair pressed her palm flat against the cold floor to steady the tremor in her hands.

A radio chirped. "Sector clear?"

The guard tapped his earpiece. "Negative. Still sweeping."

Blair exhaled through her nose. They were looking for something. Or someone. Shit. What if they knew she was here?

The moment their backs turned, she bolted for the next doorway.

A hand clamped over her mouth from behind, yanking her off-balance. She thrashed, elbow jamming backward into flesh. A grunt. Then another set of hands seized her arms, wrenching them behind her back.

"Got her."

Blair kicked, her heel connecting with a shin. A man cursed. His fist tangled in her hair, jerking her head back.

"Stop fighting, bitch," a voice growled.

She spat in his face.

The backhand came fast, snapping her head to the side. Copper flooded her mouth. They dragged her forward, her boots scraping against the floor as she struggled.

"Let go, you motherfucker. I said get your fucking hands off me—"

One of them laughed. "Yeah, that's not happening."

They hauled her through a set of double doors into a sterile white lab. The lights were too bright, glaring off stainless steel tables lined with syringes and monitors. And standing in the center, hands clasped behind his back like he'd been waiting, was Ryland.

Blair's breath locked in her chest. Every vertebrae froze.

The guards shoved her forward, and she stumbled, knees hitting the ground hard enough to bruise.

Ryland didn't move. Just watched her with that same detached amusement, like she was an experiment he'd already predicted the outcome of.

"Leave us, gentlemen," he said.

The guards hesitated. "Sir—"

"Now."

The door clicked shut behind them. Silence.

Blair's hands shook where they pressed against the floor. Her lungs refused to expand. Every scar, every healed fracture—her body remembered.

Ryland crouched in front of her.

"Becky." His voice was soft. Mocking. "I forgot how good you look in distress." He reached for her, and she flinched. His fingers brushed her jaw, tilting her face up. She recoiled, but he tightened his grip, nails biting into her skin. "Still fighting me?" He smiled. "God, I missed that."

Her pulse roared in her ears. She couldn't speak. Couldn't move.

Ryland's thumb swiped blood from her split lip. "You weren't very smart, coming here alone." His fingers dug into her arm, hauling her up so fast her vision blurred. He slammed her back against a steel lab table, the edge biting into her spine. Equipment rattled, a beaker shattering on the floor.

"Where is Tanner?"

He moved faster than she could process, his hand clamping around her neck. "What did you fucking say?" His voice was a low growl.

Blair's vision darkened at the edges as Ryland's fingers tightened around her throat. She clawed at his wrist, nails digging crescents into his skin, but his grip only tightened. His smirk never slipped.

"Where is he?" she choked out.

Ryland's thumb stroked the frantic pulse in her neck, mocking. "You mean the soldier boy who helped get you out of that warehouse?" His free hand grabbed her left hand, bones grinding together as he examined her wedding ring. "You still belong to me, Rebecca, even if you played house and whore with the big friendly giant."

"Not... yours," she managed to say.

Ryland's grip loosened just enough for Blair to drag in a ragged breath. His fingers lingered on her throat. "You still don't understand, do you?" His voice dripped with amusement. "You've always been mine."

Blair twisted in his grasp, her knee jerking up, but Ryland anticipated the move, sidestepping with a laugh and slamming her back against the table. Metal bit into her spine.

"You always were a slow learner. Maybe I should teach you a lesson like I used to."

He released her. Blair gasped, stumbling back, her throat burning. Her entire body trembled as he started to roll up his sleeves. Memories of the same action occurring before pain and pleading flooded to her mind, and every part of her screamed to run.

Blair pivoted to lunge for the nearest scalpel glinting on the steel tray. She barely grazed the handle before his fist caught her across the temple. White-hot pain exploded behind her eyes. The ground rushed up to meet her, her knees hitting the linoleum with a sickening crack.

Ryland loomed over her, rolling his wrist leisurely like he'd merely stretched before a workout. "You never could follow directions." His polished shoe nudged her ribs. "Up."

Blair spat crimson onto his pristine pant leg.

His nostrils flared. The kick to her ribs stole her breath. She curled inward, gasping, only for him to haul her up by her hair. Agony lanced her scalp.

"I said up." His fingers knotted in her hair, jerking her head back until vertebrae popped. He pressed in behind her, wrapping an arm around her torso.

Distantly, she registered liquid heat dripping down her chin—her split lip weeping onto her blouse. Ryland's breath ghosted over her ear. "This is the part where you beg."

Blair bared her teeth. "Go. To. Hell."

He chuckled, releasing her hair. His free hand slid down her side, fingers trailing down her waist until he reached her hips. When his hand travelled inwards towards her center, she bucked and reared, panic flooding through her.

"I doubt you're this much of a prude with your hulking giant." He cupped her crotch, kissing the side of her neck. "Come on, Becky, don't you remember how much fun this used to be?" His mouth clamped down on the exposed junction of her neck and shoulder.

Blair screamed as teeth pierced skin.

Ryland bit down harder, the pain white-hot and blinding. When he finally released her, she sagged, gasping. He wrenched her upright by the bicep. Tears blurred her vision, but she refused to let them fall.

"Where." She swallowed blood. "Is. Tanner?"

Ryland went terrifyingly still. His fingers tightened around her bicep hard enough to bruise.

"You want to know what happened to your precious soldier?"

"Where is he?" Blair wiped her mouth with the back of her hand, her sleeve coming away dark with blood.

"Fine." His voice dropped, smooth and dangerous. "Whitney! Get over here."

Slow footsteps came from the shadows.

Tanner emerged like a ghost—limbs moving, but his expression hollow. No recognition. Nothing. His dark eyes, usually so sharp, were empty.

Blair's heart lurched.

"Tanner—" Blair lunged forward but Ryland held her arm, fingers biting.

"You wanted to see him." Ryland shrugged. "Here he is."

Blair's pulse hammered against her ribs. "What did you do to him?"

"This?" Another casual wave toward Tanner. "Just a little trial run. The early version of VX-7 doesn't quite stick yet." Ryland sighed like it was merely an inconvenience. "Keeps wearing off every few hours. Imagine having to boost soldiers mid-battle—logistical nightmare." He stepped closer, his breath hot against her ear. "That's where you come in, darling. Your research is far more elegant."

"Tanner!" Blair tried again to get to her husband, but Ryland's grip held fast. "Tanner, look at me!"

Tanner stared straight through her.

Ryland clicked his tongue. "The serum's got a few side effects. Emotional dampening." He traced a finger down her cheek. "But don't worry—pain receptors still work just fine. And I'm fairly certain that inside that little mind of his, he's recognizing everything that's happening. His consciousness is just along for the ride now, though."

"You psychotic bastard!" Blair wrenched against Ryland's hold.

Ryland released her only to backhand her in the same movement. The crack echoed off the lab walls. Tanner didn't react. Didn't even blink. Her face hurt, ached. Her ribs throbbed within her.

Leaning in, Ryland stroked her cheek with the back of his hand. "See, this is why we always worked so well." He gripped her chin, forcing her to meet his eyes. "You fight. Right up until breaking point." His thumb swiped blood from her lip. "Then you fold. But that fight? That fire? God, I missed it."

Blair spat in his face.

Ryland went rigid. Then, slowly, he wiped the blood and saliva from his cheek. His expression darkened.

"Time for play is over. Now it's time to get to work." Ryland dragged Blair across the lab. He shoved her into a chair next to a data terminal, the Vx-7 formula glowing ominously on-screen; his failed attempts to replicate her work littered with errors.

"Remember these?" Ryland asked, producing handcuffs from his pocket. The metal clamped around her right wrist, securing her to the desk. In another life, it'd been a metal bed frame. "You're going to sit here until you fix the stability issues, making sure the effects are permanent. Just like the good wife you used to be."

"I'm not your wife."

Ryland's smile widened, and he pressed closer, his body pinning her against the back of the chair. "Legally, you are. That cute little identity swap didn't include divorce papers, Becky. In the eyes of the law, you're still Mrs. Michaelson. Still mine."

His free hand traced down her neck, lingering in ways that made her want to vomit. "I've been very patient. Very understanding about your little rebellion. But now it's time to come home and remember your place."

"Burn in hell," Blair spat, lifting her chin despite the terror clawing at her chest.

Instead of anger, her defiance seemed to excite him. "There's my feisty little wife," he murmured, his voice taking on an edge that made her skin crawl. "For a second, I wondered if that bodyguard had fucked all the fight out of you. I'm glad to see he didn't. Breaking you again will be so much more satisfying." The handcuff bit into her wrist as she tried to put distance between them, but there was nowhere to go.

"This is what you're going to fix," Ryland said, gesturing to the computer screen displaying his corrupted version of her work. "You're going to make my formula permanent. You're going to give me the missing piece that makes your compound so much more effective than mine."

"I won't," Blair said, her voice hoarse from his grip on her throat. "I refuse to help you turn people into slaves."

Ryland's cold smile was terrible as he reached into his jacket and withdrew a long, thin blade that gleamed under the harsh fluorescent lights. The sight of it made Blair's breath catch.

"You always were stubborn," he mused, testing the blade's sharpness against his thumb until a bead of blood appeared. "It was one of the things I loved about breaking you down piece by piece. But I think you'll find my methods have improved during our time apart."

Blair forced herself to meet his gaze, lifting her chin in defiance even as her heart hammered against her ribs. "You're still the same pathetic little boy who has to force people to obey you. Still not man enough to earn loyalty."

His smile widened, and terror spiked through her veins at the genuine pleasure in his expression.

"Whitney," he called in a lilting voice, never taking his eyes off Blair. "Come here."

Tanner stopped exactly two feet from Ryland's side. Up close, Blair could see the glazed quality of his eyes, the complete absence of the man she loved. It was like looking at a corpse that was still breathing.

"Take this," Ryland said, offering Tanner the knife handle-first.

Without hesitation, Tanner accepted the weapon.

"Now," Ryland continued, his voice taking on the tone of a professor giving a lesson, "I need my wife to understand the importance of cooperation." He smirked. "That ring looks awfully tight." He tapped Tanner's left hand, where their wedding band glinted. "Take it off for me. All of it."

Blair lunged against the cuff, chain rattling. "No. No, Ryland, please—"

But Tanner was already moving. He examined the simple platinum band on his ring finger, and positioned the blade just below the ring near his knuckle.

"Tanner, please," Blair begged, her voice cracking. "Don't do this. Fight it. I know you're in there somewhere."

But there was no recognition in his eyes, no hesitation in his movements as he pressed the blade down and began to cut.

The sound was wet and terrible. Steel through flesh and bone and cartilage. Blood sprayed across everything, but his face never changed expression even as he severed his own finger to free the ring.

Blair screamed, the sound tearing from her throat as she watched the man she loved mutilate himself without flinching. The severed finger hit the floor with a wet thud, the wedding ring still gleaming gold against the pale flesh.

"For fuck's sake, Whitney," Ryland said irritably, pulling out a white handkerchief. "You're getting blood everywhere. Clean the knife and give it back."

Obediently, Tanner wiped the blade on his pants with his good hand, leaving dark stains on the fabric, then handed it back to Ryland.

"Better." Ryland pocketed the knife, then bent to retrieve the severed finger. Blair watched in horror as he worked the ring free from the cooling flesh, examining the simple band with amusement glittering in his eyes.

"Bit too big for my taste," he mused, sliding the ring onto his own ring finger. It hung loose, too large for his slender hands, but he seemed pleased nonetheless. "But it'll serve as a reminder of who you belong to until I can get it resized."

Blair stared at Tanner's ring on Ryland's finger, at the way it slipped and shifted because it didn't fit properly, and felt something inside her break. That ring represented everything good Tanner had been—devoted, faithful, protective. And now it was a trophy on the hand of a monster.

"Now go get that hand treated before you bleed out," Ryland told Tanner dismissively. "Can't have you dying when I still need you."

Tanner turned and walked away without a word, without even glancing at the finger he'd left behind, blood dripping in a steady trail behind him. The man who'd taken a bullet for her, who'd made her feel safe for the first time in years, disappeared into the shadows like he'd never existed at all.

Ryland casually turned the severed finger over in his hand and examined it with the detached curiosity of a researcher studying a specimen. Then he tossed it onto the desk directly in front of Blair, where it landed with a soft, wet sound next to the keyboard.

"Get to work," he said. The stolen ring caught the light as he folded his hands. "Fix my formula, or next time I'll have him cut off something you'll really miss. His dick, perhaps. I imagine you've grown quite fond of it."

He moved toward the door. "You have two hours before his next dose. I suggest you work quickly. The longer you take, the more creative I'll get with my encouragement. Maybe I'll make him use a rusty spoon next time."

The door sealed behind him with a pneumatic hiss, leaving Blair alone with the smell of blood and antiseptic, staring at the piece of the man she loved lying on the desk like a grotesque paperweight.

For a moment, she just sat there, handcuffed to the chair, watching Tanner's blood slowly congeal on the concrete floor. Then the sobs came; great, heaving things that tore from her chest and left her gasping for air.

She'd made a mistake coming here.

CHAPTER THIRTEEN

BLAIR

BLAIR'S HANDS SHOOK AS SHE STARED AT THE MOLECULAR formula that could enslave the world. The antiseptic smell of the lab mixed with the metallic scent of dried blood—Tanner's blood—created a nauseating cocktail that made her stomach lurch.

1 hour and twenty-seven minutes. That's how long she'd been sitting here, her mind automatically cataloging the three critical errors in Ryland's VX-7 variant while her conscience screamed at her not to fix them. The neural pathway targeting was crude, amateur. The stabilization sequences were completely wrong. If she corrected just those mistakes, thousands of innocent people would become hollow shells like—

Like Tanner.

Her gaze fell on his severed finger, still lying beside the keyboard. The platinum band she'd kissed countless times was now circling Ryland's finger, a trophy of ownership that made bile rise in her throat.

The lab door hissed open.

"Time for a little progress report, Becky."

Blair's entire body went rigid at the sound of Ryland's voice, her nervous system flooding with the familiar cocktail of adrenaline and terror. Her shoulders hunched automatically.

"The formula has fundamental structural flaws," she said without turning around. "The binding affinity coefficients are completely wrong. It would take—"

"You better say another hour or two."

"Weeks. It'll take weeks to fix, Ryland." It was a flat-out lie. She could fix this. Could've already been done with it.

His footsteps echoed closer. "Is that so? But darling, I think you're being modest about your capabilities,."

How many times had he called her 'darling' right before the pain started? How many nights had she lain awake analyzing the precise moment his voice changed from loving to lethal?

"Whitney," he crooned.

Blair's heart clenched as another pair of footsteps approached. She forced herself to look as Tanner emerged into the harsh fluorescent light, his bandaged hand held carefully at his side. The same blank expression, the same mechanical posture. But for just one second— one precious, heartbreaking second—his eyes met hers.

Then the emptiness returned, and Blair had to bite her lip to keep from sobbing.

He was still in there. Trapped. Had Ryland already given him another dose?

"My wife seems to believe I'm intellectually inferior," Ryland said conversationally, his hands settling on Blair's shoulders. His fingers dug into the muscle until she winced. "She forgets that I've been studying her work for years now. Every paper, every patent filing, every breakthrough that made her so brilliantly... useful."

Blair tried to twist away from his touch, but the handcuff bit deeper into her raw wrist. "Then you understand the implications—"

"Implications?" Ryland's laugh was the same cold sound she remembered from their worst fights. "Becky, this is evolution. Imagine a military where every soldier follows orders without question. A society where crime disappears because no one can choose to commit it. Perfect order through perfect compliance."

"You mean zombies." Blair's scientific mind rebelled even as her body shook with remembered fear. "Complete neural suppression leads to cognitive deterioration. Memory loss, motor function decline, eventual vegetative state. Your 'perfect soldiers' will be braindead within months."

His fingers tightened on her shoulders, finding the exact spots where he'd left bruises during their marriage. "Then you'd better solve that problem, hadn't you?"

Blair forced herself to focus on the molecular structures displayed on the screen, her analytical mind seeking refuge in data while her emotions raged.

"Every failed iteration gets tested on Whitney first," Ryland continued, his voice taking on that reasonable tone that used to precede the worst abuse. "Every side effect, every unpleasant consequence. He's my canary in the coal mine."

"You can't—" Blair started.

"I can do anything I want." His hands slid from her shoulders to her throat, thumbs pressing against her carotid arteries. "So here's what's going to happen," Ryland continued, his breath hot against her ear. "You're going to fix the stability issues in my formula. You're going to make it permanent and elegant, just like your original work. And you're going to do it in the next hour."

Blair's throat constricted under his grip. "And if I can't?" Her breath came in shallow bursts as Ryland's grip tightened around her throat. His thumbs pressed harder against her pulse points, those elegant fingers she'd once admired now instruments of terror.

Ryland smiled—that slow, predatory grin that had haunted her nightmares for years after she'd fled. His fingers loosened just enough for her to gulp air before he released her completely and stepped back. He turned to Tanner.

"Have a seat there, Whitney," he commanded. "I want you to watch."

Tanner moved without hesitation, lowering himself onto a metal chair against the wall. His blank eyes stared straight ahead, his damaged left hand resting palm-up on his thigh.

Ryland pulled a key from his pocket and unlocked Blair's cuff before dragging her upright by her hair. Her scalp burned as strands tore away.

"There's something you've clearly forgotten since our marriage," Ryland murmured, dragging her toward the center of the lab. "The cost of disobedience."

She was already bracing by the time the first blow came; a back-handed strike that snapped Blair's head sideways. The throbbing in her head triggered the memories: The first time, they'd been on their honeymoon in a suite in Geneva. The bathroom door had locked automatically behind them. Those same long fingers wrapping around her wrists while he—

"This isn't a negotiation," Ryland hissed, kicking her knees out from under her. Blair collapsed onto the cold tile, her palms scraping against the textured safety flooring designed to prevent lab spills. Designed to protect researchers. The irony would have made her laugh if she weren't choking on terror.

Her ex-husband's expensive dress shoes came into view as he unbuckled his belt. The familiar hiss of leather sliding through loops made Blair's entire body tense. Not again. Not again. Not—

He grabbed her shoulders and flipped her onto her back, knocking the wind from her lungs. Blair instinctively curled into herself, arms crossing over her chest while her legs drew up protectively. They'd danced this horrific waltz before. She knew every step, every feint and deflection that would only prolong the inevitable.

He chuckled darkly and seized her wrists in one hand, pinning them above her head. "Are you remembering too?" Ryland mused, his free hand tearing open her blouse. Buttons scattered across the floor. "I am. Remember our second anniversary? God, that was fun."

Blair's stomach heaved. Three broken ribs that time—he'd claimed she fell in the shower. The hospital staff hadn't questioned DARPA's golden boy.

Cold tile bit into her bare back as Ryland yanked her skirt up past her hips. Blair bucked violently, her knee connecting with his thigh instead of the groin she'd aimed for. Pain exploded across her face as he struck her again—harder this time—leaving her vision swimming with black spots.

"You'll lay still," Ryland breathed against her ear as his weight settled over her, crushing her into the floor. His teeth scraped along her jugular in grotesque parody of Tanner's affectionate nips. "Whitney will watch the whole time."

"No—Ryland, stop—" She twisted, trying to buck him off, but he was stronger, his weight crushing her into the ground.

"You always fought me," he murmured, his voice almost fond. "Even when you knew you'd lose."

Not again. Not again.

Her breath came in ragged gasps, her body locking up as memories crashed over her—nights when he'd drag her out of bed, when he'd whisper "you're mine" into her skin like a curse.

"Tanner!" she screamed, her voice breaking. "Please, Tanner, help."

No reaction.

Ryland laughed. "He can't hear you. Not like this."

His hand fisted in her hair again, forcing her head to turn toward Tanner.

"Look at him," Ryland hissed. "Look at your guard dog."

Tanner sat motionless, his focus fixed straight at her, unblinking. No recognition. No anger. Nothing.

Ryland's fingers dug into her hip as he shoved her skirt up higher, tearing away her underwear.

Blair choked back a sob, her fingers clawing at the floor, searching for something—anything—to fight back with.

Then his weight shifted, and she felt the cold press of his belt buckle against her skin.

She squeezed her eyes shut.

Don't fight. Don't scream. It'll be over faster if you don't fight.

His body crushed hers, his fingers biting into her thighs as he forced her legs apart.

She screamed.

It didn't stop Ryland as he mounted her.

Blair retreated into the dark corners of her mind, where Ryland couldn't reach her. Where she could pretend this wasn't happening. Where she could pretend Tanner wasn't sitting there, watching, unable to save her, and she unable to free him.

CHAPTER FOURTEEN

TANNER

TANNER SAT MOTIONLESS IN THE CHAIR, HIS HANDS resting on his thighs, his expression slack. His green eyes didn't blink. Didn't react. But inside his skull—

I'm going to pull every fucking finger off your body, Michaelson.

The silver band on Ryland's left hand flashed under the harsh lab lights as his fingers curled around Blair's throat. Not Ryland's ring, *his* ring.

Tanner's jaw *should* have clenched. His muscles *should* have coiled. He *should* have lunged from the chair and broken Michaelson's spine over the fucking lab bench six times over. But the chemical straitjacket of the Vx-7 compound kept his body docile even as his mind raged.

Blair's face contorted beneath Ryland's grip, her lips parted on a silent gasp as Ryland forced himself on her.

Tanner's pulse *should* have spiked. His vision *should* have tunneled. Instead, his fingers stayed relaxed against his thighs, his breathing even. The pain from his left hand throbbed dully where he'd been forced to take a knife to his own goddamn finger. The stump had been hastily bandaged. Blood had soaked through the gauze.

Hold on, Blair. Hold on.

His wife's cheeks were wet. Her wrists had gone limp where

Ryland pinned them above her head. Her blouse gaped open, revealing the livid bruising already forming where Ryland had struck her.

When this wears off, I'm going to feed you your own fucking teeth, Michaelson.

But the serum held.

Tanner could do nothing but watch as Ryland grunted above her, his grip tightening on her throat. Blair's breaths were ragged hitches —too shallow, too fast. Her nails scraped uselessly at the tile floor.

Something shifted.

The barest flicker of resistance, like a muscle twitching after atrophy. Tanner could feel his fingers now—the ghost of sensation prickling at his fingertips. The serum was wearing off.

But too slowly. Too fucking slowly.

Blair's lips moved silently now. No sound came out, but Tanner didn't need to hear it to understand.

Not again not again not again—

Ryland chuckled against her jaw, his free hand fisting in her hair. "Always so dramatic."

The numbness in Tanner's limbs wavered; the chemical hold fracturing as adrenaline surged through his veins. Tanner's pinky twitched.

Ryland's cold gaze flicked to Tanner, smug. "What's wrong, Whitney?" He smirked. "Nothing to say?"

Tanner's lungs burned with the words he couldn't speak.

Your biggest fucking mistake was keeping me alive.

The monster turned back to his prey, missing the moment Tanner's head tilted to the side. His fingers twitched again.

The serum was wearing off in waves. First his hands, then his arms, his legs, his jaw. Every muscle burned with the effort of staying still while Ryland violated Blair on the cold lab floor. But Tanner didn't move. Not yet. His body wasn't trustworthy yet. But fuck, he wished it was.

Ryland's breath was ragged. Blair wasn't fighting anymore. Her eyes were closed, her lips parted in silent agony.

Hold on. Just a little longer, Blair. Just a little longer.

164

As soon as Tanner's body obeyed him, he stood. Slowly, silently, he rose from the chair.

Ryland didn't notice.

Tanner crossed the distance in three strides. His left hand—the one missing a finger—closed around the back of Ryland's neck. His right locked onto his shoulder.

He ripped the monster off Blair.

Ryland barely had time to gasp before Tanner slammed him onto the ground and straddled him. The shock on Ryland's face was almost comical; his mouth open, eyes wide.

"Whitney, stop—"

Tanner punched him in the face.

Bone cracked. Blood sprayed from Ryland's nose, splattering across his lips. He wheezed, trying to scramble backwards, but Tanner had at least six inches and an extra seventy-five pounds on Ryland. There was no getting out.

Clearly desperate, Ryland's hand shot to his knife. Tanner saw the glint of steel a second before Ryland drove it toward Tanner's ribs.

But with his body fully his again, Tanner caught his wrist

And he snapped it.

Ryland screamed, swearing profanities that somehow sounded like music to Tanner's ears. The knife clattered to the floor, and Tanner picked it up.

For the first time since this nightmare started, Tanner spoke.

"You touched my wife."

Tanner squeezed Ryland's broken wrist until the bones ground together beneath his grip. The man's scream was ragged, spit flying from his lips as he thrashed against the floor, still pinned beneath Tanner.

"You lost your right to these." Tanner bit the knife, holding it between his teeth as he used his other hand to grip Ryland's pinky. Even with the blade in his mouth, Tanner grinned as he snapped Ryland's finger to the side. One by one, he broke the fingers until they all stood out at strange angles.

Beneath him, Ryland howled, pleading and begging. Tanner

ignored him just as Ryland had ignored Blair's pleas. Taking the knife out of his mouth, Tanner cocked his head to the side.

"Watch carefully, asshole."

Tanner held the knife—the same one Ryland had handed him hours ago to carve off his own finger—and pressed the blade to the first digit. Ryland's breath exploded out of him, eyes bulging.

"Wait—wait—"

Tanner didn't wait.

The knife bit deep, severing tendon, splitting bone. Ryland's ring finger hit the floor with a wet *plink*, blood spurting from the stump. His scream crackled in the air.

The ring clinked against the floor, and Tanner dropped Ryland's hand momentarily to pick it up and remove it. "This is *mine*." Tanner slid it onto his right hand's ring finger before grabbing Ryland's injured hand again.

"Please—please stop!"

But Tanner didn't stop. Didn't hesitate. He cut through the middle finger, pinky, thumb—lining them up on the tile like twisted little trophies. Ryland kicked, sobbing, until Tanner pressed the knife flat against his broken wrist and sawed through muscle and shattered bone. When he was finished, Ryland's hand fell away completely, and he passed out.

Also-fucking-lutely not.

Tanner slapped him awake. "No," he growled. "You don't get to fucking sleep."

Ryland's remaining hand flailed, grasping at nothing. Tanner caught it, twisted, and broke the wrist with a sickening pop. He didn't let Ryland slip into unconsciousness again. Every time the man's eyelids fluttered shut, Tanner delivered another sharp crack of his palm across his face, snapping his head sideways. Blood speckled the tile, his own mingling with Ryland's where Tanner's missing finger oozed beneath the bandage. He didn't even register the pain.

"You don't get to fucking check out," Tanner snarled, tightening his grip on Ryland's shattered wrist. The man whimpered, his remaining stump of a hand twitching uselessly against the floor. "You don't get to fucking escape."

Bones cracked as Tanner wrenched the other wrist sideways again. Ryland's scream scraped raw against the lab walls, his body convulsing in Tanner's grip. The knife was still slick, still hungry.

Tanner worked slower this time—pinky first, severing it with a clean slice. The blade caught on the ring finger's knuckle, requiring a harder push, tendons snapping like overstretched rubber. Ryland's sobs turned breathless, his face mottled red and white beneath the blood. Tanner pressed Ryland's broken palm flat against the tile. The index finger came next, the knife biting through flesh with a wet *snick*.

Ryland gagged, his throat working soundlessly as Tanner tossed the fourth finger onto the growing pile. His breath hitched when Tanner leaned down, the knife's edge kissing the base of his thumb.

"This one'll hurt," Tanner murmured, and shoved the blade through. Ryland's back arched off the floor, a strangled scream tearing from his lips as the thumb rolled free. Tanner didn't hesitate. He carved through the wrist, severing the last of Ryland's hands.

Tanner wiped the blade clean against his thigh. The man was barely conscious now, blood pooling beneath him in a slick, dark halo. Tanner adjusted his grip on the knife, angling it toward Ryland's left eye—

A hand touched his shoulder.

Blair.

His attention snapped up to where she stood beside him. Her breathing was uneven, her face streaked with tears and smeared blood, but her fingers were steady when they brushed his skin, running the back of her knuckles against his cheek. Tanner stilled.

She didn't speak. Just held out her palm.

Tanner pressed the knife into it without hesitation.

Blair's grip was sure as she stepped around him. Ryland's glazed eyes tracked her weakly, his lips forming a soundless plea.

She didn't hesitate.

The blade flashed once. Ryland's shriek shattered into a wet gurgle as blood sprayed, and Tanner couldn't stop his own wince. Ryland's severed dick hit the floor with a nauseating *plop*. Fuck, his wife was terrifying. Blair kicked it aside with her toe, her face blank. She handed Tanner back the knife, and went to sit in the chair by the desk, motioning wordlessly for Tanner to continue.

God, he loved her.

Tanner gripped Ryland's chin, tilting the bastard's face toward Blair's silent, shivering form. His eyes fluttered—fading in and out of consciousness—but Tanner wouldn't let him slip away that easily. He leaned down, lips brushing Ryland's ear.

"She's fucking mine."

The knife punched through Ryland's left eye with a wet crunch. The blade scraped bone before Tanner twisted it. A shudder wracked through Ryland—half-formed scream gurgling out between ruined lips —before his body went slack, his remaining limbs splayed in surrender. Tanner yanked the knife free with a jerk, sending vitreous fluid splattering across the tile.

Silence.

Then the slow *drip-drip* from the knife. The ragged hitch of Blair's breathing behind him.

Tanner exhaled through his nose and stood, wincing as the movement jostled his mutilated hand. Blood had soaked through the crude bandage—his missing finger a dull, distant throb beneath the adrenaline. His shoulder ached too. But none of that mattered now.

His gaze locked onto Blair.

Tanner's breath came rough as he dropped the knife and crossed to her in two quick strides. His hands—one mutilated, both trembling— hovered inches from Blair's shoulders before he forced them down. No. He wouldn't be like Michaelson. He wouldn't touch her without her permission. Blood dripped from his bandage onto the tile between them, joining the mess already pooling across the lab floor.

Blair didn't speak. Her fingers curled tight around the arms of the chair, knuckles white. Her blouse hung torn at the collar, her throat blooming with bruises Tanner wished he could erase from existence.

Carefully, Tanner lowered himself to one knee before her, wincing as his injuries protested. He kept his wrists loose on his thighs, palms upturned. An offering. A surrender. "Blair." His voice crackled like broken glass.

Her breath hitched, gaze lifting to his. For an endless moment, she searched his face—the harsh lines of his clenched jaw, the blood splattered across his temple—before exhaling shakily. Her fingers unfurled from the chair, reaching for him.

Tanner caught her hand between his own before she could pull back, pressing her palm flat against his chest where his heart hammered violently against his ribs. "You feel that?" His thumb traced slow circles against her skin. "That's yours."

A soft sound escaped her—half sob, half laugh—and then her other hand was fisting in his shirt, dragging him forward until their foreheads touched. Her body shook against him, but she didn't cry. Just breathed him in.

Tanner slid his uninjured hand behind her neck, fingers threading through the tangled strands of her hair. His nose brushed hers, feather-light—unspoken permission—and when Blair tilted her chin up a fraction, he closed the distance with aching gentleness.

Their mouths met softly. This was slow. Reverent. A whispered promise beneath shattered glass and flickering fluorescents.

"Mine," he whispered against her lips. "Fucking mine."

"Fucking mine," she echoed.

CHAPTER FIFTEEN

BLAIR

BLAIR KEPT HER FINGERS LACED WITH TANNER'S UNDER the conference table, her thumb tracing slow circles over his knuckles. The warmth of his skin grounded her. It was proof he was alive. Across the polished mahogany, Carson paced like a caged predator, his tailored suit doing nothing to soften the fury rolling off him.

Benedict leaned against the window, arms crossed, watching the exchange. Jenna sat stiffly beside James, her fingers drumming a silent rhythm on the table. Penn was already buried in his laptop, likely scrubbing the last digital traces of Ryland's abomination from existence.

Carson stopped mid-stride and slammed both palms onto the table, making the water glasses tremble. "Seriously Blair? What the fucking hell were you thinking?"

Blair flinched.

Tanner was out of his seat before Carson finished the sentence, chair screeching against marble. He closed the distance between them in two steps, chest almost brushing Carson's. "Say it again." The words were quiet. Deadly. "Talk to my wife like that again."

Blair jolted up, wedging herself between them before fists could fly. She pressed a hand against Tanner's chest—his heartbeat hammered against her palm. "Stop," she murmured. His jaw flexed, but he didn't budge, glare locked over her head at Carson. "Tanner, he's right."

Tanner's gaze snapped to hers, incredulous.

"I *was* stupid. I should've waited. Should've listened." Blair glanced at Carson, whose jaw was clenched so tight she could see the vein pulsing in his temple. "I'm sorry, Carson. I apologize to all of you."

Blair's throat tightened as silence stretched between them. Discomfort prickled along her skin at the weight of their stares. Tanner remained motionless beside her, radiating silent fury at Carson's outburst. His fingers twitched against hers, just as desperate to touch her as she was to him.

Penn was the first to break the tension. He snapped his laptop shut with a decisive click. "Apology accepted." His voice was surprisingly firm for someone perpetually hunched over screens. "And for what it's worth, scrubbing those systems was child's play. Nexus might as well have left the doors unlocked." A flicker of mischief sparked in his eyes. "Lab accident's already hit the news feeds. Some faulty wiring in their neurotech bay—total loss."

Jenna stretched her arms behind her head, smirking. "My team sanitized the place before the fire. No bodies, no traces. Just another shady corp cutting corners."

James unfolded a legal document on the table. "DARPA's already spinning the explosion as a tragic setback in *their* research initiative." His smile was razor-thin. "Convenient how all their records on recent 'acquisitions' got caught in the blaze."

Blair exhaled, shoulders relaxing marginally. "Thank you," she muttered. "All of you."

"Where's Penten?" Tanner's voice was low, razor-edged.

Carson sighed through his nose and dragged a hand through his hair. "Vanished. We had eyes on him after the ambush in the warehouse, but he ghosted somewhere between Boston and Hartford. He's gone."

Tanner's fingers curled into fists. "Not for fucking long."

Before Blair could reach for him, Jenna cleared her throat.

"We'll flush him," she said, flipping open a slim tablet and sliding it across to Tanner. "Got chatter he circled back to Manhattan last night. Couple underground clinic hits near the docks—bullet wounds." Her sharp smile was all teeth. "Coincidentally matching injuries from the fight at the warehouse."

Something like amusement shifted behind Tanner's dark eyes. "They were pretty shitty shots. Of course they hit one of their own." He took the tablet, scanning the data. Blair watched his jaw work, the way his thumb tapped once—hard—against the screen. "I'll take care of him myself."

"On that happy note," Benedict said, clearing his throat. "I have good news for you, Dr. Whitney."

He produced a folded letter sealed with the Science Advisory Board's insignia. "Your lab's been reinstated. Full access, no oversight, plus an official apology for the—and I quote—'egregious mischaracterization of your work.'"

Blair snatched the document, scanning the dense legalese with widening eyes. The words *unfounded allegations* and *profound public interest* leapt out at her. She let out a sharp, incredulous laugh. "They're groveling."

Penn smirked without looking up from his laptop. "Not groveling. Covering their asses before the lawsuits hit."

Jenna tapped one booted foot. "Good luck suing ghosts. Nexus's records show they strong-armed the board to revoke your clearance."

Blair barely had time to process the victory when James cleared his throat, shifting uncomfortably in his seat. He slid a second, thinner envelope across the table. Tanner went still beside her.

"Annulment paperwork." James's voice was carefully neutral. "Predrafted when your marriage certificate was filed. Just needs signatures, if that's still something both of you want."

Blair's fingers paused on the crisp edge of the envelope. The temperature in the room seemed to drop ten degrees. Tanner didn't move—didn't even breathe, she realized—just watched her with a terrifying blankness, his usual control stretched paper-thin. She could almost hear his unspoken question: *Is this where you run?*

She yanked the papers free, scanning the first page. *Petition for*

Dissolution of Marriage. Irreconcilable differences. A laugh bubbled up in her throat. Slowly, deliberately, she turned toward Tanner's jacket, slung over the chair next to her. She fished through the pockets until her fingers closed around his silver lighter. Blair rose to her feet.

Carson's eyebrows shot up. "Uh, Winters—"

"Whitney," both Blair and Tanner corrected at the same time.

Blair dropped the entire stack into the steel trash can in the corner and flicked the lighter open. The flame caught the edge of the first page with a hungry hiss, curling black at the edges.

Benedict made a choked noise.

The fire gutted the words *null and void,* turned *spousal termination* to ash.

Blair grinned as the flames crackled higher, painting the walls orange. "There. Problem solv—"

Strong hands caught her waist. Tanner spun her around and crashed his mouth into hers before she could finish, kissing her with a ferocity that burned hotter than the annulment. His fingers dug into her hips, dragging her flush against him. Somewhere behind them, someone—Benedict?—muttered, *"Jesus Christ."* Carson groaned like he'd been punched. Penn's glasses hit the table with a clatter.

Blair barely registered any of it. She tangled her fingers in Tanner's hair, biting his lower lip in retaliation for the sudden ambush. His answering growl vibrated against her tongue. She could taste the adrenaline still lingering on his lips, the promise of *mine, mine, mine* in every possessive slide of his mouth.

A chair scraped back. "Nope," Penn declared, sounding strangled. "I'm out."

"Seconded," Carson muttered, already heading for the door.

"Expect my therapy bills," Benedict called over his shoulder as James dragged him out by the elbow.

Jenna paused just long enough to flip the conference room lights off—leaving them in the flickering glow of the dying fire—before slamming the door behind her.

Tanner didn't stop. He walked Blair backward until her shoulders hit the wall, one hand cradling the back of her head before impact. His other hand slid down to grip her thigh, hiking her leg around his hip—

The door creaked open.

"Last thing," Jenna announced. "There's a perfectly good safehouse four blocks away." A beat. "Use it." The door slammed again.

Tanner exhaled sharply against Blair's mouth, shoulders shaking with silent laughter.

Blair nipped his jaw. "Still think this marriage was a bad idea?"

He pulled back just enough to meet her gaze, eyes dark as embers. "Worst tactical decision of my life." His thumb brushed her bottom lip. "But best thing that ever happened to me."

Somewhere down the hall, Carson bellowed, "Just, for the love of god, stay out of my fucking office. I don't need to burn another fucking desk!"

Tanner kissed her again.

The fire reduced the last of the paperwork to smoke.

EPILOGUE
TANNER

RAIN SLICKED THE ALLEY'S PAVEMENT, TURNING discarded trash into obstacles slick enough to break an ankle if Tanner misstepped. But running hazards were nothing compared to Dominic Penten's refusal to die quietly. The bastard had slipped containment *three times*—once mid-interrogation, twice after the Nexus facility and Ryland Michaelson's death. Not tonight.

Tanner surged forward as Penten rounded a rusted dumpster, his breathing controlled despite the burn in his lungs. Thirty yards. Twenty.

Tires screeched. A black SUV fishtailed into the alley's mouth, blocking Penten's escape route with inches to spare.

Penten skidded to a halt. Tanner didn't slow.

He drove his shoulder into Penten's spine, slamming him face-first against the SUV's reinforced rear door. The impact jarred up Tanner's arms as Penten's skull cracked against the SUV's window. The man twisted like a cornered animal, elbow snapping back toward Tanner's ribs. Tanner pivoted, letting the strike glance off his side, and drove his knee into Penten's thigh. A grunt, but no buckle.

"Christ, Whitney," Penten spat, blood streaking his teeth as he wrenched free. "You're really still obsessed?"

Tanner didn't answer. His left hand—missing the ring finger Ryland had forced him to sever—latched onto Penten's throat while the right drew the combat knife from his belt.

Penten headbutted, and Tanner tried to dodge, but not fast enough. White light exploded behind his eyes as Penten's skull clipped his temple. The taste of copper flooded his mouth where his teeth had sliced his cheek.

Without another moment of hesitation that might give Penten a chance to escape again, Tanner rammed the knife upward.

The blade scraped past ribs, punching through muscle until the hilt met fabric. Penten's breath gurgled, his eyes bulging as Tanner leaned in, close enough to smell the acrid sweat of fear.

"Say hello to Michaelson," Tanner said. He twisted the knife.

The body slumped. Tanner caught it before it hit the pavement, grunting as he heaved Penten's dead weight into the SUV's cargo hold. Blood smeared the leather seats. He'd need to hose it down before Blair saw—no, scratch that. Blair had seen worse.

The SUV's driver-side window rolled down. A scarred hand extended, holding a damp towel.

"Damn man, you're getting slow," Jenna Briggs said.

"Fuck you, Briggs." Tanner wiped his face. The towel came away streaked pink. "I had to make sure he felt it."

Jenna's smirk was razor-thin. "You gonna dump him or bake him a cake?"

Tanner slammed the trunk shut. "North warehouse. Acid pit's still set up." He palmed his phone. One text to Blair.

Penten's done.

Her reply was instant.

Good. Don't track blood into the house.
Almost done with therapy. I'll probably beat
you home. Fajita bowls good for dinner?

He smiled and sent her back a quick response, tossing the bloody towel into the back. Tanner climbed into the passenger seat. "So, what's up with you and James? You two fucking yet?"

"Fuck you, Whitney."

———

TANNER GUIDED THE SUV THROUGH THE WINDING STREETS after he and Jenna took care of Penten's remains. The rain had thinned to a light drizzle by the time he pulled into the private drive of his mansion. He'd rarely lived there, preferring the apartment in the building near Crest Strategies. But since Blair had moved in with him, he'd enjoyed the larger space, and he'd been able to redesign the entire basement as a lab for his wife. He'd never seen her so speechless as the day he'd taken her down there and shown her all of the machines her assistant Constantine had recommended. Yeah, that had been a really good night.

Inside the sleek foyer, Tanner paused by a marble table, tossing his keys into a bowl. His muscles ached from the night's exertions. Maybe Jenna was right. Maybe he was getting slow. Eh, fuck her. He wasn't slow.

Blair glanced at him when he found her, curled up on the oversized reading lounger she'd claimed as her own in the living room. Bathed in the warm glow of a reading lamp, she seemed serene and completely at ease, absorbed in whatever scientific treatise currently held her interest. Clad in one of his comically large sweatshirts, underwear peeking from beneath, and fuzzy socks that stretched over her knees, she was hands down the sexiest thing he'd ever seen. And thank fucking god she was his.

"Hey." Her face lit up with warmth. She set the tablet down as he approached.

He leaned over, pressing his lips to her forehead. "Missed you. Let me wash off."

She smiled, a touch of mischief in her eyes. "Thank you for tying up lose ends."

"My pleasure."

"Oh, and Penn called. He said he'd text you tomorrow."

Tanner paused at the hallway door, leaning against it with his hands in his pockets. "Did he say what it was about?"

Blair shrugged, her attention already on the tablet again. "No, just said it was surveillance related."

"Huh. Okay."

Tanner took a military shower, rinsing the night away in less than two minutes, the water temperature colder than he preferred but quick to revitalize.

Resurfacing with only his boxers on, droplets still trailing down his torso, he found Blair right where he'd left her. She lifted her arm, wordlessly inviting him in. Eagerly, he stretched out, resting his head in her lap, his feet dangling off the edge of the lounger that was far too short for him.

Her fingers brushed through his short hair. She read silently, and he let himself drift, lulled by her presence—the subtle scent of her skin, the steady rise and fall of breath.

As Blair finished her article, she set the tablet aside, fingers starting to trace along his back. Each stroke relaxed the layers of tension he hadn't realized he'd carried home. He closed his eyes, something loosening deep within. Tanner felt more human than he had in years, his wife's fingers making lazy patterns across his back.

Annabelle would've loved Blair. Well, pre-abduction Annabelle would've loved her. They would've been best friends and probably would've spent hours researching together. Tormenting him together. Laughing together. Fuck, he missed his sister.

But at least he'd been able to save his wife.

He shifted slightly, propping himself on one elbow to watch her. Blair had a serenity about her that wrapped around him like a favorite childhood blanket. The way her lips curled into a smile, the soft blush kissing her cheeks—it anchored him, made him realize just how damn lucky he was to have a partner like her.

"What's that look for?" Her playful voice pulled him from his reverie. She tucked a strand of hair behind her ear.

"You, me, this." Tanner traced the edge of the sweatshirt she wore, his sweatshirt. A silly thing to be possessive about, really—from a closetful of black and gray—but on her, it was art. "And how much I love seeing you in my clothes."

Tanner let his fingers drift beneath the hem of his sweatshirt, tracing up the soft skin of Blair's thigh. The hitch in her breath, the way her lips parted—it was all the encouragement he needed. He shifted, rolling her beneath him on the wide lounger, pressing a hot kiss to her neck.

"Still sore from last night?" He asked, his mouth against her pulse.

Her laugh was breathy as her fingers tangled in his hair. "Always."

"Good." He nipped her collarbone, reveling in her sharp inhale.

His hands mapped the familiar territory of her body—the dip of her waist, the swell of her hip, the way her thigh hitched instinctively around him. He tugged the sweatshirt higher, revealing the dark lace of her panties. Lace, even when she wore his clothes. His mouth watered.

"Are you wet for me?" His thumb brushed over the damp fabric.

Blair arched into his touch. "Figured you'd check."

"Damn right." Tanner kissed her hard, swallowing her gasp as he slid a finger beneath the lace. Warm, slick, perfect. He groaned into her mouth. "Fuck, you feel good."

She bit his lip. "If you think that feels good—"

He didn't let her finish. With a growl, he slid off the lounger, dragging her to the edge. The sweatshirt bunched under her arms, baring her stomach, the swell of her breasts. His hands wrapped around her thighs, yanking her hips forward, and he dropped to his knees.

Blair's fingers clutched the cushions, her focus wholly on him.

"I'm starving," he said, watching her from between her legs.

"Then eat."

He pressed his mouth to the lace, teeth scraping the delicate fabric before pulling it aside. His tongue licked a slow, filthy stripe up her center, relishing how she shivered.

"Jesus." Her head tipped back.

He hummed against her, licking deeper, slower, savoring the way she clenched around nothing. He'd never get enough of this—the

179

sounds she made, the salt-sweet taste of her, the way her thighs trembled when he curled his tongue just right. She reached down, hands twisting in his hair as she pressed him closer. God, she could suffocate him, and he'd die happy.

He licked into her again, one hand gripping her hip, the other sliding up her stomach to palm her breast. His thumb flicked over her nipple, and she moaned, hips jerking into his mouth.

"More." The word was a gasp, a plea.

Tanner gave her more.

He sucked her clit into his mouth, swirling his tongue hard, and Blair cried out, her heel digging into his back. He held her there, relentless, until her thighs tightened like a vice, her whole body taut—

She came with a shattered moan, thighs squeezing his shoulders. Tanner didn't let up, licking her through it, drawing out every last tremor.

When she finally slumped, panting, he kissed the inside of her thigh, nuzzling the damp skin. "Lube?"

Blair's laugh was breathless. "You have to ask?" She reached into the side table drawer and pulled out a small bottle.

Grinning, he rose, gripping her waist to haul her up against him, her legs wrapping around his hips. "You just happened to have lube there?" He bit her earlobe.

"I put a bottle in every side drawer."

"God, I love you."

"I love you too." Her grin matched his as she rolled him onto his back. "Now it's your turn."

Fuck, he loved this woman.

Tanner lay sprawled across the lounger, muscles taut beneath Blair's touch as her fingers trailed down his chest. The teasing dip of her fingertips just above the waistband of his boxers sent fire licking through his veins. She knew exactly what she was doing—that smirk playing on her lips, the glint in her eyes—and fuck if it wasn't the hottest thing he'd ever seen.

His breath hitched when her fingers hooked into the elastic of his boxers, sliding them down just far enough to free his cock. The damp fabric clung briefly before Blair tugged it clear. His erection sprang free, already throbbing, heavy against his stomach. She gave him a slow, deliberate stroke from root to tip, her thumb catching the bead of precum gathered there before dragging it down his length again.

Tanner's jaw clenched. Control. He needed to control himself.

Blair smirked. He liked discipline, restraint, command... but she fucking loved breaking it out of him.

Her lips parted, tongue flicking out just once—a slow, taunting tease—before she took him deep into her mouth in one slick slide.

His fingers tangled instantly in her hair, knuckles whitening from restraint alone. She was hot velvet wrapped around him, her tongue pressing firmly along his underside as she sucked him deeper. It would have been enough—just her mouth, her hands gripping his thighs— but then she moaned around him, vibrating against his length, and his hips jerked before he could stop them.

Blair pulled back with a wet pop, flashing him a look that dared him to break.

"Are you going to let me play?" she murmured, thumb circling his leaking tip.

Tanner swallowed a curse. "You fucking know it."

"Then hold still." She grinned wickedly before dipping down again, this time swallowing him a quarter of the way, her hand working the rest of him in tight, rhythmic strokes. His control frayed with every bob of her head, every hum against his cock. She took him deeper with each pass, testing her limits, testing his, until she'd gone half- way. Her throat fluttered around him, and she gagged.

His spine arched, hips lifting off the lounger before he slammed them back down—trying, *Christ*, trying not to fucking choke her—but Blair didn't pull back. If anything, she steadied him with her hands on his hips, forcing him to stay still as she worked him ruthlessly, throat stretching around him with every slick slide.

The sight alone nearly undid him.

She pulled back just enough to breathe, saliva clinging obscenely between her lips and his cock before she dove back down, hollowing her cheeks around him, sucking him harder.

Tanner's hand tightened in her hair—not guiding, not pushing, just feeling, fingers trembling with the effort not to fuck her mouth raw.

"Blair—" His voice was ragged.

She answered by taking him deeper than before, deep throating him.

Fuck.

His release slammed into him, hips jerking uncontrollably as he came down her throat in thick pulses. Blair didn't pull away, swallowing every drop until Tanner's grip finally loosened, his breath coming harder than it had in any fight.

But he was still hard.

Blair released him with a satisfied lick, wiping her mouth with the back of her hand before climbing over him, knees bracketing his hips. She spread the lube between her hands, running them up and down his shaft twice before smearing the leftover on his chest. Tanner's fingers immediately dug into her thighs, dragging her higher until her center brushed his cock—still aching, still throbbing from her mouth.

She lined him up. For just a moment, she stayed there, elevated, just the tip of him pressing against her entrance. And then she sank down onto him with a slow, shuddering exhale.

Tanner's head tipped back, teeth grinding at the almost unbearable pressure of her swallowing him whole. Blair whimpered at the stretch, but didn't stop, sinking lower until she was fully seated, thighs trembling around him.

She leaned forward, pressing her forehead to his, breaths mingling as she adjusted. "Still think—" A shaky gasp. "Still think I can't take you?"

His answering laugh was rough. "You fucking take me like a champ."

She kissed him hard before lifting herself halfway up and slamming back down.

Tanner saw stars.

His hands flew to her hips, gripping hard as Blair set a punishing pace, riding him with reckless abandon. Every downward thrust forced a choked moan from her lips, her nails biting into his chest as she fucked herself on him.

His cock throbbed inside her, still oversensitive from his first release, but she didn't slow down. If anything, she ground deeper, eyes locked on his as she chased her own pleasure.

"Fuck—" His hips jerked upward, driving impossibly deeper, and Blair cried out, fingers twisting in his hair.

She felt it—she had to—the coiled tension in him, the way his breath came shorter with every thrust. But she didn't stop.

His orgasm built slow and brutal this time, rolling through him like thunder as Blair clenched around him, her body tightening right before she shattered.

Blair came with his name on her lips, her spine arching as she pulsed around him, milking him ruthlessly until Tanner's vision whited out. He spilled inside her with a groan, hips grinding upward to drag out every last drop of pleasure as Blair collapsed against him, slick with sweat and utterly spent.

Breathing hard, Tanner stroked her back idly, still buried inside her.

"Damn," Blair murmured against his shoulder, sounding smug as hell.

Tanner smirked, tipping his head to press his lips to her temple.

Yeah.

Damn.

READ THE FIRST CHAPTER IN THE
NEXT NOVELLA IN THE BILLIONAIRES
OF CREST STRATEGIES SERIES

A DARK BILLIONAIRE ROMANCE NOVELLA

CODED
Truths

ELORA RAE

CHAPTER 1
VICTORIA

THE CURTAIN ROSE ON THE MASQUERADE SCENE, AND Victoria melted into Meg Giry's posture—back straight, hands clasped, the perfect obedient ballet rat. The stage lights hit her like a baptism, burning away everything that wasn't this moment, this role. She could vanish here. No past, no future, just the rush of the orchestra and the electric hum of an audience holding its breath.

The sopranos hit their high notes, and Victoria spun into the choreography—feet precise, skirts whispering against her thighs. The Phantom's shadow loomed on the layered set behind her, but she didn't flinch. Stagecraft. Fake chandeliers, fake danger. Nothing like the real thing.

A collective gasp rippled through the crowd as the Phantom's noose snapped tight around Buquet's neck. Victoria let her own breath hitch—Meg was supposed to be afraid, and god, it felt good to let fear be pretend. When stagehands yanked the prop body into the flies, she let a tremor run through her arms. Someone in the wings murmured, "Damn, Omstadt sells it every night."

Easy when you've practiced.

She pirouetted into the next formation, sweat prickling at her temples under the wig. The spotlight found her. Not her, though. Meg. She was Meg.

When the final curtain fell to thunderous applause, Victoria held her pose—Meg's wide-eyed innocence—until the houselights killed the magic. The illusion shattered. Shoulders dropping, she peeled off the character like a second skin as the cast dissolved into chatter and sweaty hugs around her.

Backstage smelled of rosin and hairspray, the air thick with the collective exhalation of twenty performers shedding their roles. Victoria navigated the maze of props and cables with muscle memory, her body still humming with leftover adrenaline. For three hours, she hadn't been the girl with the clenched jaw in grocery store lines, or the woman who triple-checked her door locks. She'd been Meg—sweet, uncomplicated Meg.

The collective dressing room was a sanctuary of cracked mirrors and wilting bouquets from well-wishers. Tonight, a new arrangement sat atop her vanity: white peonies wrapped in brown paper, their petals trembling when she shut the door behind her. No ribbon, no card—just a slip of paper tucked between the stems.

"Your Meg makes them forget Christine exists."

Victoria's fingers hovered over the note. Eleven performances just this month, eleven bouquets. Always peonies. Always unsigned. It'd been that way since her very first show four years ago.

A giggle burst out of her. Backlit by the vanity bulbs, the flowers glowed like stage lights. The Phantom sent Christine roses; her phantom sent peonies.

She tucked the note into her script and reached for the cold cream. In the mirror, her reflection flickered between gratitude and unease. Gifts meant attention. Attention meant being seen.

But for the length of the overture, the length of an aria, she wanted to be seen, even if she had to go back to invisibility afterwards.

The peonies trembled as she wiped away Meg's blush. The dressing room door banged open, releasing a burst of laughter and the smell of perfume. Christine flounced in, her silk robe gaping as she shoved sweaty dark curls off her forehead. "Queen Meg strikes again!

Bet they're giving you my role next season." She grinned, ripping off her petticoat like a bandage.

Victoria chuckled, massaging cold cream into her cheeks. "Wouldn't that be a twist?" The familiar script of backstage banter had her grinning. "But you can keep Christine. I love Meg."

"And she loves you, V." Madame Giry swept in next, still stiff-backed even as she peeled off her gloves. "Your footwork during the ballet was immaculate tonight." She squeezed Victoria's shoulder as she passed to her own vanity.

Other chorus girls trailed in behind her, chattering about post-show drinks. One elbowed Victoria's shoulder. "Coming tonight?"

"Raincheck," Victoria said, snapping her makeup case shut. "Early call tomorrow with my mother."

"Oh, you're no fun." The flock of them dispersed in a flutter of wet wipes and costume bags.

Victoria pulled off the wig cap, shaking out her real hair—a deep auburn this month—then scrubbed until her skin burned pink. In the mirror, Victoria Omstadt emerged inch by inch until Meg was just a smudge of glitter under her nails. She changed into her oversized hoodie and sweatpants, lacing her tennis shoes tightly.

The backstage lights dimmed as the last of the cast trickled out, their laughter echoing down the hall until it dissolved into silence. Victoria lingered, the only sound being the soft creak of her chair as she leaned back. Her fingers traced the edge of the vanity, where the peonies sat, their white petals stark against the cluttered surface. Her reflection stared back with tired green eyes. She looked like herself now, whoever that was.

The note still tucked in her script stared up at her. She pulled it out, smoothing the creases with her thumb. The handwriting was so neat it almost looked printed. Maybe it was. She'd spent a few days the first time the flowers arrived four years ago trying to figure out who had sent them, but gave up when she found nothing. It had unsettled her at first. All the others received flowers from friends, family, and fans. It was normal. But for her, because of her past, it had felt... threatening. But they kept coming, and not once had the person revealed themselves. Four years of performances nearly every night, flowers, every night.

Whoever was sending them had money to burn, it seemed.

Victoria folded the note and slipped it into her bag, standing to grab her coat. With another glance around the room to make sure she'd picked up all of her belongings, Victoria flipped the light switch and left out the side door.

The alley behind the theater was a canyon of brick and shadow. She hated it every night. Her sneakers scuffed against the pavement, the sound swallowed by the city's hum. She pulled her hood up, her breath visible in the cold. The streets were quieter now, but not empty. A cab hissed past, its headlights cutting through the dark. Victoria's fingers tightened around her keys, one poking awkwardly between her knuckles. The streetlights buzzed overhead, throwing long shadows that stretched too far—like someone could step out of them at any second. Baby hairs on the nape of her neck prickled.

She glanced back. Nothing. Just the usual graffiti-scarred walls and the distant laughter of strangers spilling out of a bar. But the feeling clung anyway, sticky as sweat.

Victoria quickened her pace.

Twenty steps later, the air shifted behind her. A scrape of a shoe she hadn't seen coming. She whipped around.

Empty sidewalk.

Her pulse thrummed. Could've sworn—

No. Nothing.

The fluorescent glow of a bodega flickered ahead like a beacon. She crossed the street without checking for traffic (there was never traffic at this hour, but she always checked—always—except tonight, when her body was already moving before logic kicked in). The door chimed as she shoved inside.

"Evening," the clerk mumbled without looking up from his phone.

Victoria grabbed the first thing her fingers touched—spearmint gum—and slapped it onto the counter. Her reflection in the security camera footage looked warped.

She forced her fingers still as she fished out a crumpled bill.

"That all?" The clerk asked, still not looking up from his phone.

Victoria pressed her lips together and pocketed the gum she didn't want. "Yeah. Thanks."

The bell jingled again as she stepped back into the dark.

Her apartment was three blocks away. Three. She exhaled through her nose and started walking; fast enough she wouldn't have to hear footsteps behind her, slow enough she wouldn't look like she was running.

A shadow moved where it shouldn't. Across the street. Between parked cars. Victoria froze.

The streetlamp caught pale fingers retreating into the dark. The glimpse vanished so fast she couldn't be sure she'd seen it at all. But she had. She knew she had.

Her reflection flickered in a shop window as she passed; her face pale, her shoulders tense. The shadow behind her was just a blur, but it was there. She ducked into a narrow side street, her heart pounding. The footsteps paused. Then they stopped.

Victoria held her breath, pressing herself against the wall. When she finally dared to peek around the corner, the street was empty. Just the glow of a streetlamp and the distant rumble of the subway.

She exhaled, her breath shaky. Victoria forced herself to keep moving, her pace steady now, her keys still clenched in her fist. The city loomed around her, its windows like unblinking eyes. She didn't look back.

The security gate to her apartment building screeched shut behind her, the metallic clang loud enough to make Victoria flinch. She pressed her palm against the door until she heard the lock click, her shoulders finally dropping a fraction. The lobby smelled of stale takeout and lemon floor cleaner, the flickering lights buzzing like an angry fly. Up the stairwell she went—always the stairs, never the elevator—her tennis shoes silent against the chipped concrete steps.

By the fourth floor, her calves complained, but the ache was welcome. She fumbled with her keys outside 4C. Inside, nails scrambled against hardwood.

"Hey, baby." She crouched as Sandy barreled into her, tail thumping, wet nose pressing into her collarbone. The dog's whole body wriggled—too big to be a lapdog, too small to be intimidating, but her warmth seeped into Victoria's bones like sunshine. She buried her face in Sandy's golden fur, inhaling the familiar scent of dog shampoo and the faint musk of home. "Missed you too, girly."

Victoria shrugged off her bag, letting it slump onto the armchair. The peonies went into a chipped vase on the kitchen counter, their petals already unfurling in the warmth. Her fingers lingered on the stems as she plucked the old bouquet—slightly wilted, edges browning—and dumped it into the trash. Every surface held flowers: a bouquet on the bookshelf, another on the nightstand, and yet another near the bathroom sink. All from him. Her phantom.

After she closed the blinds and the curtains for good measure, Victoria checked the door was locked and started getting comfortable. Peeling off her sweatshirt and bra with a sigh, Victoria traded them for an oversized NYU T-shirt that swallowed her frame. The sweatpants followed, kicked carelessly toward the laundry basket. Cool air kissed her bare thighs as she padded across to her kitchenette. The studio apartment wasn't large, but she'd made it Sandy and her home.

Popcorn rattled in the microwave, kernels bursting one by one. She poured herself a generous glass of red—the cheap kind that came in a large box—and curled onto the bed. Sandy flopped beside her, immediately commandeering half the pillows.

"Annie, 1982," Victoria told the screen as she queued it up. The opening credits blared, and Sandy perked up at the familiar tune, tail thumping against the comforter. Victoria grinned, scratching behind her ears. "Yeah, yeah, I know. Your namesake."

Halfway through "Maybe," her phone buzzed. Clara's face flashed on screen—her sister's freckled nose scrunched in a smirk, braces glinting. Victoria swiped to answer.

"You watching it too?" Clara's voice crackled through the speaker. On her tiny screen, TV light flickered across Clara's face, the same opening scene playing behind her.

Victoria held up her bowl of popcorn in salute. "Obviously."

Clara rolled her eyes but snuggled deeper into her blanket cocoon. "You're so predictable."

"Says the person also watching it." Victoria took a slow sip of wine, studying her sister's face—the dark circles under her eyes, the way her fingers picked at her cuticles. "Rough week?"

Clara hesitated, then shrugged. "Geometry test. Ms. Gerard's a killer."

Victoria frowned. "You studied, though. You'll crush it."

"I dunno. I blanked on the practice exam."

"Hey." Victoria waited until Clara met her gaze through the screen. "You're smarter than you think. And if Gerard fails you, I'll make her disappear."

Clara snorted. "You'd get caught in, like, five minutes."

"Three, max."

Laughter burst out of Clara, and Victoria's chest warmed. They settled back into the movie, occasionally mouthing along to lines in unison. Comfort in the shared ritual.

"I should get to bed," Clara mumbled when the credits rolled, already half-asleep.

"Text me after the test," Victoria whispered. "And no caffeine past eight, or you'll be wired."

"Yes, *Mom*."

The call ended, leaving the apartment too quiet. Victoria set the phone aside and stared at the blackened screen. Sandy whined, nosing her elbow.

"Okay, okay." Victoria scratched behind her ears again, but her gaze drifted to the window. The blinds were shut tight. No gaps. No shadows. And even if there were, her curtains were a second set of protection.

So why did she still feel watched?

READ THE REST OF PENN AND VICTORIA'S STORY IN THE NEXT BILLIONAIRES OF CREST STRATEGIES NOVELLA:

MAKE SURE TO CHECK OUT
ALL FIVE BOOKS IN THE
BILLIONAIRES OF CREST STRATEGIES SERIES

ACKNOWLEDGMENTS

I somehow published another book. If you're reading this, it means *Salvaged Vows* exists in the world, which feels both surreal and slightly concerning given how dark this one was. This is Book Three. I should probably have more chill about it by now. I absolutely do not. If anything, my mind is even more corrupt than it was before.

First, thank you to my parents, who have now accepted that their daughter writes about emotionally unavailable men with violence as a love language. They've stopped asking when I'm going to write "something nice" and have moved on to just hoping I don't get put on a government watchlist. Fair concern, honestly.

To my brother, who definitely hasn't read this one either (smart choice), but continues to tell people, "My sister's got this whole series going," with the kind of pride usually reserved for actual accomplishments. His brotherly love is what inspired Tanner's love for Annabelle. You're the best hype man a girl could ask for.

To my beta readers: Dani R., Mariah S., Rachel H., and Zoe M. - thank you for diving into Tanner and Blair's chaos with me. Your notes in the margins helped me refine a lot of mess. You all deserve hazard pay for the emotional whiplash.

Writing *Salvaged Vows* was like performing surgery on my own feelings while blindfolded. Publishing it feels like handing you the scalpel and hoping you don't run. Thank you for trusting me with your book boyfriends and your bookish hearts.

Thank you for reading, for screaming in my DMs, and for understanding that sometimes love looks like a marriage of convenience and revenge served bloody.

Stay unhinged,

Elora Rae

P.S. Reviews are like tactical intel to Tanner... He analyzes every single one. Don't leave him hanging...

ABOUT THE AUTHOR

Elora Rae is a longtime lover of dark romance, drawn to stories about morally grey men, obsessive love, and twisted secrets. When she's not writing, Elora is probably re-reading her favorite villain origin love stories or plotting the next emotionally delicious downfall. These books are just the beginning.

www.ingramcontent.com/pod-product-compliance
Lightning Source LLC
Chambersburg PA
CBHW020415150626
46554CB00014B/1635